LOST BULLET

For Shetal, who volunteered her name

KKINGFISHER
a Houghton Mifflin Company imprint
222 Berkeley Street
Boston, Massachusetts 02116
www.houghtonmifflinbooks.com

First published in 2005
2 4 6 8 10 9 7 5 3 1

LIBRARY OF CONGRESS CATALOGING-IN-PUBLICATION DATA
has been applied for.

ISBN 0-7534-5830-6
ISBN 978-07534-5830-3

Printed in India
1TR/1104/THOM/(MA)/90GSM

LOST BULLET

MALCOLM ROSE

KINGFISHER
BOSTON

Also available in the TRACES series:

Framed!

Chapter One

The white boy walking along Tottenham Court Corridor spotted a tree snake in the elder plant growing up the side of a house. He was about to move on, staying away from it, when he was distracted by a small piece of paper that fluttered out of an upstairs window. Pushed along by the breeze, the piece of notepaper sailed straight toward his head. Owen grabbed it in his fist as if he'd caught a moth that was threatening to land on his face. Immediately, there was a scream. "White scum!" It was so loud, so angry, and so high-pitched that Owen could not even tell if it had come from a man or a woman. He wasn't going to hang around to find out who had shouted because he recognized pure hatred in that voice. He shoved the piece of paper into his pocket and ran.

On both sides of Owen rampant ivy, elder, and clematis were choking the buildings. The rifle poking ominously out of the window above and behind him was camouflaged by the masses of leaves. When Owen heard the first shot, he let out a frightened yelp and ducked. Covering his head with his hands would have been useless against the bullet if it had been on target, but it thudded into the trunk of the elm tree just to his right. Refusing to freeze with fear, he dashed away quickly.

Weaving his way down the windy London corridor, swerving around the trees that had pushed their way up through the tarmac, he tried to make it difficult for the sniper to get a clear shot at him.

The second bullet ricocheted off the ground in front of him and to the left, but the third caught his hand. He cried out in pain but did not dare stop. Cradling his injured left hand in his right, he stumbled on toward the intersection. In a few seconds he could turn on to Oxford Freeway, safe from the person with an itchy finger on the trigger. As he dodged around another tree, a window shattered with the force of the next stray shot.

Once, before Owen was born, Oxford Freeway had been busy with automatic cabs, its walkway bustling with pedestrians. But no one had been employed to maintain it—or any of central London's routes—so nature had reclaimed lost territory. The cabs' onboard computers, equipped with the latest artificial intelligence, soon learned to avoid the center of London because it became impossible to negotiate the erupting trees and shrubs. Besides, too many passengers and pedestrians were mugged in those parts to risk it.

Owen knew Oxford Freeway only as a concrete and wildlife jungle, the natural habitat of rats, snakes, and crooks. Still, until bullets learned how to turn corners, he could escape in the neglected freeway.

At the sound of another gunshot, two red squirrels darted up an old elm tree. At once, Owen felt his right foot give way as if someone had kicked it out from under him. He gasped and faltered, yet he experienced no pain. He expected to cry out in agony when he put his weight back on that leg, but he felt only some extra pressure on his heel. The bullet had hit the tarmac, bounced up, thudded into the sole of his shoe, and come to rest harmlessly in the thick layer of rubber.

Desperate to stay on his feet, Owen staggered to the intersection with Oxford Freeway. Two small patches of ivy clawing up the closest house exploded, revealing red bricks underneath. Chest heaving, Owen darted around the corner, where he was shielded from the rifle fire. Yet he did not relax or slow down. He scurried along the corridor in case the sniper came out of hiding and tailed him. Avoiding the tangle of overgrown vegetation, he raced as fast as he could, still clutching his bleeding left hand, until he got to Wardour Walkway. Turning left into the narrow passage, he zigzagged through the warren of alleys to lose anyone who might try to follow him.

The stiffening breeze pushed him through the jungle of Soho, along with masses of fallen brown leaves. He emerged at Haymarket and headed for Whitehall and the Thames river. If he could pick a safe path over the crumbling Westminster Bridge, he could admit himself to Thomas's Hospital and get his hand fixed. The hospital had a reputation for not asking too many awkward questions before offering treatment. Owen glanced nervously behind him, but the place was almost deserted. Of course, it wasn't really deserted. It was just that, for their own protection, many people stayed behind locked doors—or at least out of sight. Anyway, Owen couldn't see anyone carrying a rifle. He dropped to walking pace, limping slightly because of the lump of metal embedded in the heel of his shoe, and made his way toward the Thames.

On the riverside a group of people had hijacked a narrow cargo boat that should have been cruising sedately through the city, programmed to ignore London and deliver its goods to the heart of England. The goods on this particular autobarge would feed and clothe London bandits, not the plush Midlands. Picking his way carefully across the run-down bridge, Owen looked down at the thieves shouting to each other below him on the South Bank. One boy stood out from the rest because he was completely bald. No doubt the bandits would have time to empty the boat because The Authorities were never in a hurry to deal with petty theft in London.

There was a burning sensation in Owen's left palm. As far as he could tell, the bullet had gone straight through the fleshy part between his thumb and forefinger. Like everyone else who ventured into central

London, Owen had been injured a few times, but he had never been shot before. It was a new and painful experience. It had taken him by surprise also because he had become skilled at avoiding crime, especially muggings, along the London corridors.

Those outbursts of violence were often caused by people who were terrified of London's reputation. When they went out, they armed themselves with a hefty piece of metal or wood for self-defense.

Conventional firearms were popular for leisure activities, but in the corridors they were not common. The stinger—an electric stun gun—had become the bandits' weapon of choice. The person on the other end of that rifle wasn't a traditional mugger. It could have just been someone who was insanely protective of his property, but Owen had never been targeted on Tottenham Court Corridor before. It could have been someone who had decided to take potshots at passersby for fun, but the taunt about the color of his skin made Owen believe that he'd been singled out.

Waiting in a hospital cubicle, encircled by flimsy curtains, Owen dug the scrap of plain white paper out of his pocket and held it in his right hand. Someone had written "72 Russell Plaza," in blue ink, on a page from a notepad. That was it. Nothing else. There wasn't even anything on the other side. Owen shrugged, and when Dr. Suleman entered, he slipped the note back into his pocket without another thought.

The doctor turned her nose up at the sight of her patient. "Oh dear," she muttered.

Owen was not sure whether the doctor was referring to his injury, his genetically flawed skin, or his rough appearance. For a second he thought that he saw disapproval in Dr. Suleman's eyes. At least it wasn't the prejudice of the person who had hoped to bury a bullet in Owen's heart or head rather than his hand and heel. Owen held up his blood-encrusted hand and said, "It's a bullet wound."

"Oh dear," Dr. Suleman repeated. Gingerly, maybe even reluctantly, she examined the damaged palm but did not ask why Owen had been shot. "It looks worse than it is." Talking to a hidden computer, she called for a scan and then watched a three-dimensional skeletal image form in the air just in front of her. She walked around the hologram, studying the wound carefully from all angles, and then announced, "You're lucky."

"I am?"

"It could've been worse. The bullet's nicked a bone, but it'll heal on its own. I can give you a local anesthetic, clean it up, and sew it back together. You'll be fine." She paused before adding, "I don't suppose you've got an identity card, do you?"

"Do I need one? Not sure where mine is."

The doctor shook her head like an instructor

confronting a hopeless student. "Never mind," she said as if she'd rather report him to The Authorities.

In Owen's mind her tone confirmed it. The doctor disliked his lifestyle rather than his color. "Thanks," he said, ignoring her anxiety.

While she worked on the wound, Dr. Suleman asked Owen where he had been attacked. "Tottenham Court? I'll watch that on the way home."

"Don't think you'll have the same problem," Owen replied.

"Why's that?"

"Likely it was a brown supremacy thing."

The doctor nodded knowingly but said nothing.

Owen decided to leave the spent bullet in the sole of his shoe, where it would be his secret memento of a daring escape from a crazed sniper. With a bandaged and throbbing hand, he walked away from Thomas's Hospital. Just along the bank the bandits were still emptying the barge that they had commandeered. The blustery wind was threatening to develop into a full-scale storm. Glancing up at the bad-tempered clouds that were gathering in the dark sky, Owen grimaced. It was time to find shelter.

Once Anna Suleman used to flash her identity card past the freeway reader, state her home address, and then jump into a cab. As soon as she was seated, the computerized cab would take off along Westminster, over the bridge, and seek out a passable route on the corridors running north. Now it was useless to call for one. She hadn't seen a vehicle between the hospital and her home near Regent's Common for years. Instead she walked. If her partner was working the same shift, they would walk together. Now that cabs avoided the place, they had a choice of paths. They could stay on the intended walkways, they could use the large freeways that had both walkways and corridors, or they could trudge along the disused corridors, where walking used to be forbidden because of the danger from high-speed cabs.

Today, after her shift at Thomas's Hospital, Dr. Suleman stepped out into the dusk alone and was drenched almost immediately. The November downpour had begun in style. The thirsty vegetation relished the driving rainfall, but Anna cursed. As she walked toward the bridge, she blinked over and over again to try to keep her vision clear and to stop the wind and raindrops from stinging her tired eyes. All that she could see, though, was mist. There was possibly something to her left, a sudden movement like a shifting shadow, but then it was gone. Perhaps it was a trick of the storm.

It was hopeless. She could not walk through this weather. She spun around and headed back for the hospital entrance. It was then that the shape returned—definitely this time. It was a figure, striding toward her, holding . . . something. Anna squinted her eyes, but it was like trying to see a bat flying across the night sky. "Is anybody there?"

The slippery figure had vanished again. There was nothing but the ferocious sound of the angry cloudburst. The closest lamp was flickering on and off. Probably water was getting inside it and wreaking havoc with the electrical contacts. The rest of the lights were battling to keep night at bay but succeeded only in illuminating countless raindrops.

"Alex? Is that you?" Anna called.

This time there was an answer. "Are you a doctor?"

Dr. Suleman stopped and shouted in the direction of the voice, "Yes. Are you hurt?" She wiped her eyes. "Where are you? What do you want?"

Lightning punctured the air. Anna heard one more word before the thunder deafened her. "Respect!" Through the deluge she could barely see the person who had spoken. She certainly didn't see the rifle. Engulfed by nature's fierce roar, she could not distinguish the explosion of the storm from the brutal blast of the weapon.

Chapter Two

The worst of the storm and gusting wind had passed. In a persistent drizzle Forensic Investigator Luke Harding and Malc were examining Dr. Suleman's sodden, lifeless body by the southern bank of the Thames river. Some water dripped down from a large cherry tree and plopped onto Dr. Suleman's still chest. That regular pulse of rainwater had replaced her heartbeat, adding to the misery of the murder.

The Authorities had erected floodlights at the front of Thomas's Hospital. The whole area glowed like the setting for a nighttime tennis match.

Surrounded by crime-scene tape, Luke let out a long sigh. At the age of 16, he was already an expert at investigating death, but he was not hardened to it. "A doctor," he muttered. "What a waste."

The hospital had downloaded details of the victim into Luke's Mobile Aid to Law and Crime. "Anna Suleman," Malc reported. "57 years old, educated at Liverpool Medical School. She never became a specialist. Instead she worked in deprived areas, first in Oxford and then here in London. In Liverpool she was paired with Dr. Coppard. He also works at Thomas's Hospital."

The rainfall had cleaned the head wound of its blood,

so Luke could see immediately what had happened. He winced at the damage that a high-velocity bullet inflicted on a human head. Not coping well with death, he shielded himself from his real feelings by following a mechanical routine.

"Check me, Malc," Luke said. "First, the entrance wound. No smoke stains or powder burns. There's a slight abrasion collar around the hole caused by the bullet's heat and friction on the skin. This wasn't point-blank. It's a medium-range shot."

"Confirmed," Malc replied. "I estimate it was fired from 13 to 30 feet away, possibly a nine-millimeter bullet."

Luke moved around to the other side of Anna's head, glanced briefly at the huge exit wound, and turned away. "It's easier to look at things like this when it's just pictures in school."

Malc was merely a machine, immune to emotion. "This is a large cavity typical of a high-velocity bullet fired from a rifled weapon impacting on a skull and then traveling through a dense organ like a brain."

"I guess it's all pictures to you, isn't it? It doesn't matter if it's a figure in a database or something you've recorded at a crime scene. It's all pictures to be analyzed and compared."

"Correct," Malc answered unashamedly.

Needing to continue with the uncomfortable job,

Luke asked, "Where's the bullet?"

"A preliminary sweep for metallic objects indicates that it is not in the immediate vicinity," Malc replied.

Luke wiped his face free of rainwater. "There's no point doing a chemical analysis for discharge residue. It will have long since washed away. Scan for 100 feet from here, looking for anything significant but especially the spent bullet, empty cartridge case, the weapon, or more bullet damage. Within 15 feet, where the killer probably stood, make it a more detailed search."

Luke was not hopeful. Anna Suleman's head was just a few inches away from a drain. The downpour had probably swept the bullet away forever, and the torrent could have carried the empty cartridge case a long distance. It might even have followed the bullet into the sewer system. Luke assumed that the culprit had taken the firearm away, and any residue would have been removed by the storm.

Malc returned and reported after seven minutes. "An autobarge is moored in the river. It has been intercepted and looted. There is nothing else of particular significance, but I have recorded all artifacts."

Luke shrugged. "I'd better take a look at the boat in case Anna disturbed the bandits and one of them shot her, but I was hoping for something more conclusive."

"I suggest you note the positioning of the drain relative to the head of . . . "

"Noted already," Luke said, water spraying from his lip. As Malc had not detected any other bullet damage, the killer had fired only once. Luke was annoyed that he was not going to recover the single bullet. He could have matched the markings on it with a particular firearm, and if he could then link the weapon to a user, he had the murderer. A spent bullet at the scene of a shooting was always a major piece of evidence, so Luke was frustrated that he had failed to find it. Annoyed, he muttered, "The rain's dissolved any decent evidence or carried it away."

"I have observed that humans have considerable capacity to complain about rain."

Trying to cheer himself up, Luke retorted, "At least I can't get rusty."

"Neither can I. I am made from a new alloy that . . . "

Luke interrupted. "Joke, Malc. Anyway, because you're just a machine, you won't mind if I send you into the sewers to hunt for the spent bullet, downstream from here."

"No. I am not affected by germs, rats, and dirt."

Luke smiled. "Just teasing. The drain's completely gushing. I can hear it from here. It's probably drowned all the rats. The bullet and anything else wouldn't stand a chance. They'll have been swept away to who knows where by now."

"I confirm that retrieval is unlikely."

"If you take her body temperature, you're going to tell me you can't estimate the time of death from it because of these conditions."

"Correct."

"When did she finish work?"

"Five o'clock this afternoon. Two hours and 12 minutes ago."

"So she probably died as soon as she left, just after five." Unwilling to accept that the crime scene was not going to yield anything helpful, Luke said, "There's got to be something here. Her clothes and bag aren't disturbed, so it's not a traditional assault or robbery." He shook the worst of the water from his hands, bent down, and opened Anna Suleman's shoulder bag. Taking a peek inside, he exclaimed, "There's enough in here to start a war. Chloroform spray—straight from the hospital's pharmacy, no doubt. A stinger and heavy club. She didn't mess around, did she? London muggers wouldn't stand a chance. Her identity card's still here, so it's definitely not a robbery." A doctor's identity card would be highly prized by a thief. Luke reasoned that any bandit would have taken it as a passport to privileges and goods.

Standing up again, Luke blew a raindrop from the end of his nose. "Well, okay, there's not much to go on. Let's go inside. For starters, log on to the hospital computer, Malc." Seeing the pager that was attached to

Dr. Suleman's waistband, Luke said, "I bet you can do it through radio contact with her pager. Get a record of the last . . . say . . . 50 patients she saw. If she couldn't help one of them . . . well, you never know. Maybe it's unlikely, but one might have a grudge against her."

Chapter Three

In the hospital lobby Malc waited while Luke shed his waterproof coat like an insect breaking free of its pupal case. "Are you allowing removal of the body?" the mobile asked.

"Yes. Get the hospital's pathology department on the job. Let them get wet for a change. I want all her clothes and possessions sent to my room." He peered around and then said, "Have you got that list of patients?"

"Confirmed," replied Malc. "But it is not complete. It seems that patients with trivial complaints are not entered into the electronic database. There may be some paper records on them instead."

"Give me a summary of the ones you've got."

Malc recited names and medical conditions rapidly. He always delivered facts at a rate that was carefully adjusted to match Luke's ability to absorb them. Toward the end, though, Luke lifted a hand and said, "Hold on."

"I assume that means you want me to stop."

"You said Dr. Suleman's last patient had a gunshot wound to his left hand."

"Correct. Owen Goode."

"That's quite a coincidence. Two people shot, same hospital, same day. I want to talk to him right now. Where does he live?" asked Luke.

"No address listed."

"Great!"

"That must be one of your ironic 'greats'."

"You're getting the hang of this, aren't you?"

"I am programmed to help as much as possible," Malc replied dryly.

"Do you have anything else on Owen Goode?"

"No."

"That's what you call helpful, is it?" Before Malc could reply, Luke said, "Did the hospital keep the bullet?"

"No. It was not in the wound."

"Where exactly was Goode when he got shot?"

"Not recorded," Malc replied.

"So, if he told Dr. Suleman, that information's died with her."

"Correct."

"Great," Luke repeated. "Oh well. First thing tomorrow, when I've got daylight, I'll check the barge. For now, I'm going to ask around about Anna Suleman."

Head in his hands, Dr. Coppard was sitting mournfully in the staff room. He looked up at Luke, apparently startled by the forensic investigator's appearance, and shook his head. "It's awful. Really awful. I didn't know I'd feel like this. I'm shocked. I've been with Anna for a long time. I feel . . . devastated. I

feel like I've lost part of myself."

Luke was touched. After pairing a couple would have two children, fulfill their parental duties by delivering them to a school at the age of five years old, and then provide each other with companionship until old age. Couples often talked about loving each other, but real love was not part of the deal. The arrangement was more about convenience. But, unless Luke was being taken in by an act, Dr. Coppard appeared to be heartbroken. "I'm sorry," Luke said inadequately.

Dr. Coppard's head drooped again, showing the bald patches among his thin, silvery hair. He would be 57 years old because Pairing Committees always selected couples of the same age. Through his sorrow, he whispered, "What do you want, Investigator Harding?"

"I need to know if Anna was in any kind of trouble here at work or at home."

"No. What do you mean?"

Luke shrugged. "Anything. Like, was she easygoing, or were there arguments, professional disagreements, or jealousies, that type of thing?"

"Nothing out of the ordinary," Dr. Coppard answered.

To Luke, that meant that there had been some conflict. "Tell me about it. I know it's a difficult time for you, but if you want me to catch whoever's responsible . . ."

"Are you fully qualified?" Dr. Coppard asked. "You look very young."

Luke waved toward Malc, inviting the computer to respond.

"Forensic Investigator Harding graduated from Birmingham School with an unprecedented set of grades. At 16 years old, he is lacking in experience but is exceptionally qualified. At this time, his success rate is 100 percent."

Dr. Coppard nodded. "I just thought . . . "

Luke interrupted. "It's all right. Back to Anna. I take it that there were some disagreements."

"It was a girl who came in. She was petrified, below the age of pairing, but she had baby twins. On top of that, there were . . . complications."

"Complications?"

"The twins—boys—were conjoined. They faced each other, with their heads only a few inches apart. Of course, they couldn't walk, so their legs were wasting away. They shared a liver between them, but luckily there were two sets of veins and arteries."

"I can see that there'd be a medical problem, but where's the clash?"

"The hospital's supposed to tell The Authorities about unlicensed children. The manager—Alex Foxton—refused. As always. He says everyone deserves help whether they're on the right side of the law or not. He

told Anna to go ahead with the operation."

"What did she do?"

"She did what she was told. The liver's an organ that regenerates. She dissected it and gave half to each baby, hoping that they'd both regenerate the rest."

"And did they?"

"As far as I know, the mother and twins are doing fine. At least they were when they left Thomas's Hospital. They haven't been back."

"What about Anna's relationship with Alex Foxton?" Luke enquired.

"Frosty. They've never got along. Foxton is unorthodox and a real menace."

Luke didn't speak. He presumed that there was more to come.

"Let's face it," Dr. Coppard added, "Foxton hates Anna for some reason. I don't know why." He buried his head in his hands again, and his shoulders shook.

Luke decided that this was not the right time to press him. He stood up. "Did she say anything about treating a patient named Owen Goode? He also had a bullet wound."

Dr. Coppard shook his head. "She's . . . she was a surgeon, but the hospital's not overflowing with doctors. She helped out with accidents and emergencies."

"Okay." Luke often asked key questions in a casual

way as if the subject was of no great concern. He wasn't sure if the operation on the twins was important or not, but he disguised his interest anyway. "I don't suppose it matters, but what was the mother's name? The one with the separated boys."

"She didn't have an identity card, but it was . . . er . . . Toback. Sarah Toback."

Chapter Four

Forty-five Visionaries sat on four long wooden pews in front of Ethan Loach and a knotted rattlesnake. The room was decorated with religious symbols and was dominated by an enormous painting of God. It was the usual clean-shaven image. He was a sympathetic figure, open palms displayed, yet commanding and a little frightening at the same time. Anyone gazing on that brown face could imagine his loving expression turning to anger and retribution at any moment.

On God's behalf, Ethan was releasing a torrent of words as harsh as the earlier rainstorm. The assembled Visionaries had heard it all before, of course, but like children with a favorite bedtime story, they never got tired of hearing it again. "What do Rationalists say? Once there was nothing. Nothing at all. Then there was a Big Bang, and a whole universe appeared. They claim a universe—yes, a whole universe, my friends—grew out of nothing at all! Yet Rationalists tell us now that you can't get something from nothing. Everything that moves or lives or breathes has to be fueled by something." Prowling back and forth, Ethan stepped over the curled snake and said, "So what fueled the start of the universe? The people who claim to be rational say it was . . . absolutely nothing. Before the Big Bang there was utter nothingness, they say. Well, let me tell them. That's not rational. You *don't* get something from nothing. Something had to fuel the Big Bang." He stared at his audience and nodded smugly. "We know what it was."

In the congregation Rachel Toback, Samuel, and at least two other Visionaries murmured, "God."

"Yes, God! God was that something before the Big Bang. Yet all those unbelieving Rationalists out there can't see what's obvious, can't see what's really rational. First things first. God was first. He was the energy. God is still our energy. He made the universe, our world, and he made us in his own image."

Outside, the small park enclosed by walkways had expanded so much that it was taking over the entire plaza. Brick, concrete, and tarmac were no match for living wood, roots, and shoots. Several buildings were showing alarming cracks and gaps in their brickwork. An extension to the building next door had lost its grip on the original building and had broken away, showing the innards like a bad wound.

Inside the London chapter of The World Church of Eternal Vision the snake's gray rattle poked out from the folds of its body as a warning. It was identifying itself as one of God's poisonous creatures, not to be messed with.

Ethan flung out an arm in the direction of the large

painting. "God is brown! Whites are not made in his image. They are nothing but genetic mistakes. Just as we are perfection, they are imperfection, an abomination. We denounce the white curse. And if their houses go up in flames, so be it. That is God's will."

"Amen!"

Ethan was a commanding figure, tall and muscular. Like the rest of the men in the room, he was clean shaven. More than that, he was almost hairless. "How can we improve on perfection, my friends? We can't. Mere humans do not have the right to interfere with perfection. No one has the right to interfere with us. Yet doctors do it all the time. They presume to interfere with the good work of God." He beat out a rhythm with his right fist on his left palm as he spat, "That is an absolute lack of respect."

Nodding vehemently, Rachel Toback muttered, "Respect!"

"That's right." Ethan hesitated and then laughed as an amusing thought came into his mind. "If God had meant for us to meddle with our insides, he'd have made our skin see-through, not brown. But he didn't, did he?" Ethan waited for the laughter and murmurings to die down. "But we have to remember something. We may be perfection, but we are only human. That means we're sometimes weak. We sin. And when we sin, we are given illnesses." Glancing at Samuel and Rachel, he said, "We know this, don't we? But we also know when we get sick, we ask for forgiveness and place ourselves in his hands, not the clumsy hands of doctors with their evil knives and machines.

"Sometimes God will cure us and sometimes not." Ethan's eyes lingered for a while on Reece, with his damaged foot. "Sometimes we learn our lesson best when he decides that we should live with our sickness—our punishment—until our bodies die. It's a sin not to trust God's judgment. If it is his will that any of us should bear a lifelong disfigurement, so be it. It's a sin to risk our souls by giving ourselves to doctors. I tell you, my friends, we have every justification for smashing their hospitals and offices. They have brought it on themselves by their disrespect to God. They work against him while we live in harmony with him."

Ethan bent down and slowly maneuvered his face close, very close, to the poisonous rattlesnake. In a quieter but even more dramatic voice he said, "Do you think doctors, whites, or the unfaithful could ever enjoy this degree of harmony with one of God's fiercest, most deadly creatures? Of course not. It won't strike me down, this snake, famed for its aggression. No. The angels protect the righteous. It won't attack me because we are both at one with God and nature."

The snake was light brown with dark diamond shapes running down the length of its long body. With its

tongue flickering in and out of its mouth, it raised its head and examined the human being that was breathing the same air. The reptile seemed more curious about Ethan than annoyed. It was used to seeing Visionaries close up. It was used to acting as the Church's test of its faith. Its warning rattle remained silent.

The leader of the London Visionaries stood tall again. "Ah, if only I could get a doctor in here to try that." He shook his head and smiled broadly. "God would use his snake to strike back at wickedness. No doubt he would decide that there should be one less doctor in the world."

"Amen."

"There are others who dare to intervene where only God and nature should go. When The Time comes, there are those who presume to know who should marry who." His laugh was angry. "They call themselves Pairing Committees. Pairing Committees! God and love guide our feelings toward each other and our choice of mates. It has nothing to do with an absurd committee."

"That's right."

Wagging his finger, Ethan continued with a scowl on his face. "Those who arrange marriages are the scum of God's world. We must use every available opportunity to remind them—and remind everyone who is living in sin—that they are an insult to God." Ethan paused before concluding his familiar sermon in a frenzy. "My friends, we may be small in number compared with Rationalists, we may be an illegal organization, but God never said anything about the majority inheriting the earth. Only the righteous will do that, and sometimes the righteous find themselves in a minority, against the law and The Authorities. So be it. The law and The Authorities are nothing in comparison with the might of God's law." He finished with both arms in the air, his head thrown back, and his eyes closed.

"Amen!"

Chapter Five

Luke did not doubt Alex Foxton's passion for Thomas's Hospital and its patients. The manager made it clear that his first duty was to the sick. He was adamant that the hospital would treat anyone without question, and he had instructed his staff to follow his policy. He certainly didn't care if, in the process, the hospital sometimes trampled over the law.

"You'll remember Sarah Toback," said Luke. "A patient with unlicensed conjoined twins. I'd like to hear about that."

Frowning, Alex hesitated for an instant. "Just what are you investigating: me and my hospital or Anna Suleman's murder?"

Luke shrugged. "I can't tell the difference at this stage, so I'm looking into anything and everything."

Alex looked startled. "You don't think I killed her, do you?"

"I can't say you didn't."

"That's ridiculous! My whole life's been dedicated to curing people, not killing them."

Luke had already noted that. "So, if Malc scanned your hands, arms, and chest for gunshot residue, he wouldn't find any."

Alex held out his arms. "Feel free."

Malc moved in, swept the beam over the manager, and, after a few seconds, announced, "No residue detected."

Luke nodded and then continued. "Tell me about the Toback business. You clashed with Dr. Suleman over it."

Alex sighed and then shrugged. "Okay. It's true we didn't see eye to eye on it. I'm the type of person who cuts through obstacles and gets things done, gets patients back on their feet. Anna was always quoting rules and telling me that we didn't have the resources. 'We can't do that because . . . whatever.' That's no way to run a hospital. It's no good reporting unlicensed births—like she wanted to do—when the babies are desperately in need of our help. You don't need an identity card to get into my hospital, Investigator Harding. You just need to be sick. We're healers, not the eyes and ears of The Authorities. Sorry, but that's just the way it is. I'm proud that my hospital gave the Toback boys a decent life."

Every five seconds a drop of leaking water formed on the windowsill and plopped noisily into a bucket of water below. The wooden window frame was rotten, and the paint on the wall around it was blistered and peeling.

Luke decided to push his luck. "I heard there was more to your relationship with Anna than that."

"Than what?"

"Than a disagreement over unlicensed twins."

"Well, maybe," Alex replied hesitantly. "We have a history, I guess. She kept an electronic diary of all of her grievances against me, and I caught her when she was about to transmit it to The Authorities—an obvious attempt to undermine me. We . . . argued."

Luke was not convinced that the manager was telling the whole truth. "Is that all?"

Alex nodded. With a weak smile, he remarked, "Not a motive for murder."

Luke assumed that he had not yet heard the full story. "You really disliked her. Why?"

Alex wore a look of innocence. "I just told you."

Luke realized that he was not going to get any further for the moment, so he got up. "Oh. Just one more thing. You come from Newcastle, according to my database," Luke said, glancing toward Malc as the computer recorded the interview. "It's got a great reputation for producing top athletes, especially in shooting."

"So?"

"You must have done some shooting yourself."

"Yes," Alex responded. "But I didn't like it. I was always more interested in patching people up than putting extra holes in them."

Not knowing how long Luke would be stationed in London, The Authorities had provided him with a suite of rooms in the Central Hotel in Piccadilly. One room had been converted into an office and mini laboratory. Even though Luke had settled into the suite, he did not feel at home in the South. He was restless and lonely.

In Birmingham he'd been surrounded by friends and the sounds of school. He could visit Jade whenever he wanted. In London he only had a tin ball—or a flattened sphere made from the best modern nonrusting alloy, packed with electronic gadgets—for company. He always seemed to be on edge, especially after dark. It was much quieter than Birmingham, and lawful nightlife seemed to be nonexistent. If London had ever had legitimate evening activities, they had long since fallen into disrepute. Most of the time Luke could busy himself with his investigation, but when the day was over, he felt abandoned.

Every time a branch scratched against his window, every time he heard the ghostly footsteps of another guest, every time an animal cried out, Luke became alert and tense. He could turn on the telescreen and catch up on the news, listen to music, or watch a movie, but there was no one to join him. He was missing so many things but friendship in particular. Malc's fantastic new alloy did not come close to the comfort of flesh and blood, but the floating computer was Luke's lifeline back to the North.

"Connection to Jade Vernon, please," he requested.

Within seconds, Jade's buoyant voice boomed out of Malc. "Hi there!"

"Hi. How's Sheffield treating you?"

"It's beautiful. And you wouldn't believe the equipment I've got. For audio, it's ten-and-a-half times better than Birmingham. And . . . I shouldn't go on. How's being an outcast down south, FI Harding?"

"About as good as you said it'd be," Luke admitted. "London's sort of evolving from city back into countryside. But the work's fine. Very good, in fact."

Malc threw Jade's image onto the telescreen. She had straightened her hair, but in color it was as chaotic as ever. It was bronze with streaks of copper and pink. On screen, her brown eyes looked gray, but the sparkle was still there. Besides, Luke preferred a two-dimensional close-up of her attractive, plump face than no view at all.

"Another creepy murder?" she asked.

"Yes."

"Oh, Luke." She didn't have to say anything else. Her regret at Luke's chosen path was absolutely clear.

Changing the subject, Luke said, "Are you making new friends?"

"Yeah. I'm tripping over them, there are so many. Actually, I'm going out with some of them in a minute."

"I see," Luke replied, hiding his regret. "Any . . . special friend yet?"

"No." Jade hesitated for a fraction of a second before adding, "There's a Pairing Committee up here looking into my situation."

"Oh." Suddenly, Luke felt like a pawn rather than a forensic investigator.

"They know all about me from Birmingham, and I've told them about you. There's not much else I can do."

"No, I guess not."

"What about you?"

"I've got a virtual meeting with the London Pairing Committee tomorrow afternoon."

There was a brief pause in their exchange, like a moment of silent respect for their suffocated, expiring relationship. Then Luke said, "What's all this equipment you've got there?"

"Well, you really should see it for yourself. A studio crammed with computers, samplers, and an archive of just about anything ever recorded. I've got the technical workshop I used to dream about."

"Sounds great."

Toning down her smile, Jade said, "Is London as horrible and primitive as it's cracked up to be?"

"It's a bit . . . raw, but it's got its good points," Luke said, eliminating every trace of the lie from his voice.

"Oh? Are you going to give me a list?"

Luke could make people believe anything he said, but Jade was the exception. She could always tell when he

wasn't being truthful. Even so, he continued with the pretense. "You haven't got long enough before you're going out with your Sheffield buddies."

"Hey. How about a visit up here? You'll love it in Sheffield, and I can play you my latest stuff. It'll be a good break for you."

"If only. Not in the middle of a murder case, Jade. Maybe when I've wrapped it up."

"See you tomorrow night then."

"Hmm. Not sure about that."

"Okay," said Jade. "I'll download some music into Malc. Something special for you. If you want."

"Of course I want. Thanks. That'll be great."

"What would you like? Chill or thrill?"

"Either. Both would be good."

"I'll get on to it. Good night."

"Have a nice time," Luke replied.

He watched her image fade to nothing, and then he turned away from Malc. For a moment he became a normal 16-year-old boy again.

Chapter Six

After the previous day's deluge the London walkways were warm and steamy. And, as always, they were claustrophobic. Above the sign that read "Venomous Snake—Warning" a green tree snake was sleeping on the bough of an elm. London was not infested with snakes, but the invading vegetation provided a lush home for several species. Some occurred naturally, while some were escaped pets that had established themselves in the wild. Most were harmless, but a few were poisonous. Thomas's Hospital had a specialist antivenin unit to treat the unwary and the unlucky.

Luke Harding and Malc went straight past the hospital, straight past the weather-beaten bunch of lilies that marked the spot where Anna Suleman died, and headed for the looted autobarge on the South Bank.

It seemed to Luke that Anna liked to report misconduct. If she had seen the thieves taking the goods, maybe she would have tried to report them. Then a bandit might have put an end to her interference with a rifle.

Even in London, Luke did not carry a weapon. Malc was his weapon. Because the Mobile Aid to Law and Crime was his constant companion, always floating nearby, it would be obvious to anyone that Luke was an

investigator. Any attack on him would be recorded by Malc, and the robotic computer would simply track the offender until backup from The Authorities arrived. That threat of any attacker getting caught was Luke's best defense. Even so, a suspect had assaulted Luke during his first case, and any forensic investigator in the South was going to face danger at some point. Before leaving Birmingham Malc had been modified to be more than a deterrent. He now had a defensive and offensive capability.

When Luke walked over the gangplank, a fat rat ran in the opposite direction on one of the thick ropes that anchored the narrow cargo boat to the cracked concrete dock. Luke didn't need his identity card to get inside. The door had been ripped off its hinges.

Luke liked it best when his feet were on solid ground. The barge was not rocking much from side to side, but he found its unpredictable little shifts unsettling. There did not seem to be anyone else on board. The thieves had had their fill and abandoned the boat to rats and snakes. He opened up the cargo hold to find that it had been completely cleared. There were not even any empty packing cases.

Luke sniffed the air and said, "Malc, analyze that smell, will you?"

"It is a complex mixture containing acetaldehyde, limonene, 2-furylmethanethiol, diallyl disulfide, benzaldehyde, and hydrogen cyanide . . . "

"Cyanide?" Luke was startled by the mention of the poison.

"It is present at too small a concentration to be dangerous. Benzaldehyde and hydrogen cyanide are aroma components of cherries and almonds. Several ripening fruits give off traces of acetaldehyde. Limonene is the odor of oranges, diallyl disulfide of garlic, and 2-furylmethanethiol of roasted coffee beans."

"So you're telling me the barge was carrying fruits, nuts, and that kind of thing."

"Confirmed."

"Were there any pomegranates?" Luke asked with a grin.

"I have not detected any chemicals specific to pomegranates."

"Anything apart from fruits, nuts, garlic, and coffee?"

"There are traces of hydrogen sulfide, ammonia, and butanedione."

"I remember butanedione. Cheesy, isn't it?"

"It is characteristic of cheese and butter, but I suggest that, when it occurs with hydrogen sulfide and ammonia, its source is likely to be the axillary region of human beings and their intestinal gas."

Luke grimaced. "You're saying it's the bandits' armpit smell—and worse."

"Correct."

"Yuck. Maybe they were hoping to steal some deodorant."

Luke moved forward to the control room. A gray drizzle that threatened to turn into another downpour obscured the view of the river through the window. Even the boat's computer had been ripped out. Luke examined the brass plate on the wrecked control panel and said, "It's autobarge 0579, Malc. Look it up later, and find out what else it was carrying." He glanced around and said, "Are you scanning all of this?"

"Confirmed. There is so much evidence that I am in danger of overload. I have recorded hundreds of fingerprints, hairs, fibers, shoe prints, plant matter, small objects, and other artifacts."

"I bet that there'll be a thousand irrelevant things and one vital . . . "

"Speculation," Malc replied.

"Yeah, well, log it all. Just in case. Then I'm out of here. It won't bother you, but I like the ground under my feet to stay still."

The mini laboratory in his hotel suite was not fully equipped for forensic examinations, but some basic apparatus that he needed was there. Item by item, he was going through Dr. Suleman's possessions and getting more and more disheartened. "All I'm getting from this is the fact that Anna Suleman was a doctor who intended to get home in one piece." Once again, he picked up her pager and looked at it through its evidence bag. "Hold on. This looks more complicated than ones I've seen before. It looks like it's got a transmitter in addition to a receiver."

Malc established a radio link with the pager and, after a minute, said, "Correct. All hospital staff carry this type of always-on pager. Each one continually tracks the location of its wearer and transmits a position signal to the hospital's central computer."

"Interesting. What time did Anna's pager stop moving around yesterday afternoon?"

"5:13."

Luke smiled. "Log that as the time of death." He brushed a big, ugly fly off his desk.

"You should note that the main hospital computer also registers when two or more such signals are in close proximity."

Luke sat straight up. "It gets better. You're saying the hospital logs the time and date whenever staff wearing pagers get together?"

"Correct. It is essential information if it takes a while to establish that a patient is infectious. The medics taking care of that patient may catch the illness and pass it on, but all of their contacts can be traced very quickly and isolated or treated to stop the spread of the disease."

Luke nodded. "I like it. Check the hospital log for 13

minutes past five yesterday afternoon. Were there any other pagers near her when she was shot?"

"No."

Luke sighed. "That's a shame. If there had been one 15 feet away, I'd have this solved."

"Irrelevant," Malc replied.

"I know," Luke said. "The system doesn't even prove that another member of the hospital staff wasn't around at the scene of the crime. If a doctor wanted to murder her, he would've taken the precaution of leaving his pager behind."

"He or she."

"Yeah, I know, but I can't keep saying that. When I say 'he,' I think 'he or she,' It's usually a 'he,' though."

"Of all solved murders, 84.7 percent were committed by males," said Malc.

"All right. I'll give him—or her—a code name. That'll help. From now on, he's . . . Lost Bullet. And, if Lost Bullet's one of the hospital staff," Luke reasoned, "he would've left his pager somewhere so it would be stationary."

"I have already checked for pagers that were motionless between five o'clock and 5:15. All doctors' pagers were moving at the time of death."

The fly that had settled on Luke's hand began to annoy him. He flicked it away. "Would it be easy to hack into the system and give a pager a new history?"

"Extremely difficult. It is a secure system."

"So, if Lost Bullet wanted his pager to move around when he was outside with a rifle, it would be easier to attach the pager to an unsuspecting person, let it hitch a ride, and reclaim it later."

"Speculation."

"True. What about Alex Foxton? What was his pager doing at the time?"

"He is not a doctor. His pager was stationary at his desk."

"Which doesn't necessarily mean Alex Foxton was also at his desk."

"Correct. However, I did not detect gunshot residue on his hands or clothing."

"He could've worn a medical gown or a coat—and washed his hands thoroughly afterward." Barely pausing, Luke said, "Anyway, download something into case files for me, please, Malc. I want to know which members of staff met Anna Suleman in the last week, where and when."

"Processing."

"Right now, I need to test your new capability. You see that fly buzzing in the window? Zap it, will you?"

Malc maneuvered himself into the ideal position, three feet away from the target. A narrow red guide beam pinpointed the insect perfectly, and then Malc fired the miniature laser. Immediately, it boiled the fly's

innards, and the exploded fly fell dead onto the windowsill.

"Thank you. Test completed. Your system seems to be working fine." Luke paused before asking, "Have you got the contents of that looted barge yet?"

"Confirmed."

"Give it to me then."

Malc hesitated, apparently unsure about Luke's request.

"I don't mean I want you to supply me with the fruits. I want to hear a list of the cargo."

"Do you wish to know quantities or simply identities?"

"Just tell me what was on it."

"The cargo consisted of pineapples, cherries, plums, mangoes, apples, oranges and kumquats, coffee, peanuts, Brazil nuts, and almonds. There were miscellaneous nonfood items: shoes, sheepskin coats, compact discs, chairs, toasters, and kettles."

"No garlic?"

"No."

"Interesting." Luke got to his feet. "Right. I'm going to Anna's apartment. I want a copy of her electronic diary—the one with all of her grievances against Alex Foxton."

Chapter Seven

As Luke walked toward the exit the hotel receptionist called after him, "FI Harding." The man's jet-black hair and beard were immaculately trimmed and groomed. "I'm sorry—so sorry—but we don't have any more pomegranates. The chef says you ate the last one this morning."

Returning to the desk, Luke asked, "Didn't you order some more?"

"Yes. Days ago. But the chef says we're always at the bottom of the list in London. Never a priority. Sorry, sir."

Luke looked down at his nameplate. "All right, Mr. Morgan. Leave it to me."

"Can you get some?"

Luke smiled. "I've got an idea."

Mr. Morgan's expression changed from panic to pleasure. "We'd be so grateful, Forensic Investigator."

A mist as dense as smoke blew down the freeway. It smeared anything in its path with moisture. All of the buildings on the way to Regent's Common were saturated. Here and there, Luke had to walk through huge puddles. Only the plant life was refreshed by the endlessly soggy conditions. Everything else looked dull. Water was running down Luke's raincoat and soaking into his pants. With his hood pulled up, his top half was dry, but his legs felt like they'd been wrapped in a cold, wet sponge. His shoes were waterproof, but his feet were still damp because rain had seeped from his pants inside his socks.

Trying to cheer himself up, he said, "Malc, I need to do some urgent forensic tests on pomegranates. Order me a crate from a reliable Birmingham fruit supplier. High priority. Get them delivered to the hotel today or tomorrow at the latest."

"Transmitting. What are the tests, and how do they relate to the case?"

"The tests mostly involve eating. And they relate to the case because I'd dissolve in the rain if I don't have one for breakfast."

"There is no link between pomegranate consumption and solubility."

Before Luke could reply, he spotted movement out of the corner of his eye. On his right two men and a boy aged around 12 had come out of an alley on to Great Portland Corridor. Without coats, they were drenched to the bone, and their saturated hair was flattened against their heads. The men's straggly beards were dripping wet. All three were carrying sharpened metal poles—possibly railings. They were about to rush across the corridor toward him, grasping their makeshift weapons like spears, when Malc positioned himself in front of Luke. At once, one of them cried, "No! He's an investigator!" They turned around and ran back down Clipstone Walkway.

Luke shook his head. "Just think what it's like for all those people who aren't investigators." Saddened by the level of hostility on some of London's routes, he continued toward Regent's Common. "You can see how it happens, can't you? Someone gets attacked with a stick, so the next time they go out they carry something better than a stick, something sharp that they can throw. To outdo that, the next one in the chain carries a gun. Then it escalates to a stinger."

Luke paused. "It could've been a random killing that got Anna, you know. As simple and awful as that. Maybe Lost Bullet thought she was a threat."

"The victim was not holding a weapon at the time of death."

"True," Luke replied. "But everyone seems so edgy here. Maybe they don't wait to see a stun gun or a club."

Reaching Marylebone Freeway, Luke stopped and asked, "Which way?"

Malc was equipped with a highly detailed map of London. He could guide Luke to any address. "Left for 230 yards. Building on the right."

Anna Suleman and Dr. Coppard lived in a giant concrete tower on the freeway. Luke had chosen to pay a visit while Dr. Coppard was out, working his shift at

the hospital. The outside of the tower was decorated with graffiti, clematis, and ivy in equal measure. After swiping his identity card through the security reader Luke entered the living quarters. By London standards, the inside was well kept, and the elevator was working. Apartments on the north side overlooked Regent's Common, and south-facing quarters like Anna's had a view over the downtown area.

Up on the 11th floor, Luke should have been able to see the full extent of London's urban decay, but heavy cloud cover obscured the distance. Even so, he could see how nature's green and brown colors had trespassed on the man-made reds and blacks. Freeway signs and walkway lamps had been pushed to crazy angles. Most of the nearby corridors were blocked with shrubs and trees. Displaced by roots, cobblestones jutted up like rows of uneven teeth. On the other side of Marylebone Freeway birds flew out of the broken windows of a building that was in the grasp of a plant that Luke did not recognize.

The files stored on Anna's home computer were protected by a password, but that did not hinder Luke. The Authorities required most software to be manufactured with security systems that could be bypassed by mobile aids to law and crime or when a computer was presented with a forensic investigator's identity card. Luke used his power of access to print a hard copy of Anna's diary and then left without showing it to Malc.

On the way to Thomas's Hospital two boys with shaved heads came up to him at Haymarket. They were around 11 years old, clearly unarmed and friendly. They were carrying only a stack of wet leaflets. The first boy said, "You're not an investigator."

"I'm not? How do you know?" Luke replied with a grin, pleased to discover that not everyone in London was itching for a fight.

"Too young."

"You might be right. But, if you are, I must be brilliant at making robots." He nodded toward Malc. "This one's not bad, but he goes berserk every now and then."

"Really?"

"Mmm. Totally and completely out of control."

The boys looked at Malc nervously, thrust one of the pamphlets into Luke's hand, and then ran away.

"Why did you not tell them the truth?" asked Malc.

Luke shrugged. "For fun, I guess."

Browsing the leaflet that was entitled "God is Brown," Luke groaned. Muttering to himself, he said, "Religious white-hate propaganda." He would have thrown the pamphlet away in disgust, but instead he shoved it in his pocket. He decided to get rid of it in the hotel's garbage can rather than litter the freeway with

such literature. He wished that he could banish senseless prejudice just as easily.

Luke sat down in Alex Foxton's office with the printout on his lap and said, "Anna's diary has got some interesting stuff in it. Very juicy."

"You've been digging around." Alex did not look like a man who had been found out. He was ready to defend his actions. "What are you going to do with it?"

Luke felt uncomfortable. In every complaint that Dr. Suleman had made against her manager Luke would have sided with Alex. It was clear from the examples in Anna's diary that Foxton cared for people. He insisted that his hospital would treat the homeless, the unlucky, and the crooks in exactly the same way that it treated people who could produce a valid identity card.

Luke forced himself to say, "I haven't allowed Malc to read it yet, but that's what the law tells me to do."

"Then what happens?"

"Malc, if you scanned this and spotted some illegal practices, like treating a wanted criminal or unlicensed children, can I instruct you to delete it?"

"No."

"What would you do with it?"

"My programming would require me to transmit it to The Authorities."

"And I can't stop that?"

"No."

Butting in, Alex said, "Okay, okay. I get the picture. You want something from me in return for not force-feeding your computer with incriminating data."

"To be blunt about it, yes."

Alex sighed. "What do you want?"

"The full story about you and Anna Suleman."

Alex sat back and let out a long, weary breath. "All right. But I want you to know that this isn't my doing. You're forcing it out of me."

"Go on," said Luke.

Chapter Eight

Under pressure from Luke, the hospital manager looked older than his 50 years. "It's all so sad," he began. "And I really don't want to make it worse for Anna's partner or put a stain on her memory but . . ." He shrugged helplessly. "I guess you were bound to find out anyway. The disagreements I had with Anna were only a symptom of what was really going on." He gazed at the pager on his desk rather than looking up at Luke. "You see, Anna fell for me some time ago—as soon as we met after I got this job. She . . . er . . . she's been bothering me ever since. I think the law would call it stalking. I put up with it for quite a long time, but I thought it'd be best to have it out with her and put an end to it. I told her straight."

"Told her what?"

"I didn't share her feelings."

"Does Dr. Coppard know about this?"

"No. He thinks he's got—I mean, he had—a loving wife. And I have no wish to disillusion him."

Luke asked, "What happened?"

"It all turned sour after that chat I had with her. I guess she held a grudge against me for . . . you know . . . not being interested. That's when she started picking fights and documenting her grievances against me." He nodded toward the diary. "I suppose she was trying to get back at me."

"Did anyone else know about this?"

"A nurse or someone might have noticed the strange looks she gave me, but I don't think so. I'm not in the business of humiliating people in public. I kept it to myself. It was between me and Anna. That's all."

There didn't seem to be any point in checking the story with Dr. Coppard. Luke was not going to find any solid evidence to prove whether or not Alex Foxton had told the truth. It was down to Luke's judgment, and Luke chose to believe him.

Luke sat in his hotel room while rain pelted the windows, blurring his view of Green Common. "You can't say I'm overflowing with suspects or clues," he said, partly to Malc, partly to himself. "Alex Foxton doesn't have much of a motive. He didn't kill her to stop her from stalking him because he'd already dealt with that. And I bet he's tough enough to handle the hassle she was putting his way. On top of that, if he's half as sincere as he seems, he's not a murderer. I doubt if Lost Bullet is as dedicated to human health as Alex Foxton is." Luke paused and then added, "Dr. Coppard's a suspect, though. If he had found out that Anna was chasing someone else, being unfaithful, he would've been very hurt. Maybe that's grounds for a crime of passion. I bet

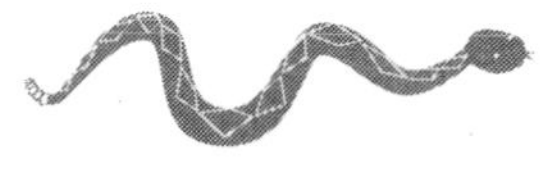

he could love her and kill her at the same time. And he'd be devastated by it."

"Speculation."

"Exactly. What I need is evidence. My best lead's probably Owen Goode—the patient with a hole in his hand. He might've seen someone in the area with a rifle. But how do I get ahold of him? Plug yourself into the London network, Malc. I'm going to need information—and lots of it."

"Standing by."

"I want you to run a full search for anyone named Owen Goode on every accessible database. Births, schools, pairings, health, deaths, crimes, anything."

"Processing."

While Luke waited his brain wandered back to the striking case of the mother with the conjoined twins. "I wonder what it's like to be a twin." Glancing at Malc, he added, "You've got many twins—in a way. Every investigator has got one of your twins."

"Correction. A twin is one of two identical, similar, related, or connected units. It is not possible to have many twins. The definition requires a pair."

"Yeah. Okay. But you know what I mean. Right now, linked to the network, you're like a conjoined twin."

"It is an unhelpful comparison. My capabilities are increased by the connection. A conjoined twin's capabilities are reduced."

When Malc had first been built, he'd been identical to every other mobile constructed to the same specification. But his programming allowed him to learn and adapt to Luke's way of working. Like a human, his experiences were shaping him, making him unique. Luke certainly regarded Malc as an individual.

"While you're logged on check out Sarah Toback, too, will you?"

"My systems are fully occupied. I will process the additional task when I have spare resources."

After another five minutes Malc reported. "First search completed. Within the parameters you set, there are three people named Owen Goode."

"Ah. Give me their jobs, ages, and districts where they live."

"Computer technician, aged 34, Tower Hamlets. Secretary, aged 42, Bexley. No job, aged 15, no address."

Luke smiled. "Who got himself shot? I'll give you one guess."

"I do not guess."

"Figure it out. Two of them would've showed up at the hospital with their identity cards. If either of them had been shot, Thomas's Hospital records would've had much more on file. It's the boy. What have you got on him?"

"Very little. There is no record of him after his birth. I have located only his name, date of birth, parents'

names, and color."

Luke looked puzzled. "Color?"

"He is described as white."

"White," Luke muttered thoughtfully. He went to his coat, fished around in a pocket, and dragged out the white-hate leaflet he'd been given at Haymarket. He slapped the sodden paper and said, "I don't understand this stuff. It's silly. What difference does color make? It's just skin. Jade would still be Jade even if she was green—like her name. And her hair sometimes."

"Prejudice against whites and albinos is very uncommon, according to statistics."

Luke was examining the small print on the pamphlet. "According to The World Church of Eternal Vision, whites are an abomination. Their whiteness is an extreme disfigurement handed down by God for an extreme sin committed by the very first white." He looked up and said, "And there was me thinking it was a harmless genetic difference." Shaking his head, he put the pamphlet down. "If Lost Bullet shot Owen Goode, it wasn't part of a war on whites because he went on to shoot Anna Suleman and she's brown. Unless the campaign includes doctors who've treated whites. Just in case The World Church of Eternal Vision's got something to do with this, Malc, search for information on it. And check records for crimes against white people. I want to know if there's any kind of pattern to it."

"I have now collated information on Sarah Toback."

"Let's hear it."

"Again, there is very little. She died one month ago at the age of 18. An investigation concluded that it was an accidental death in Euston Plaza following a snakebite. There was no evidence of murder."

"I thought Thomas's Hospital had an antivenin unit."

"To be successful, antivenin has to be administered within an hour or two. The body was found in a disused building roughly three days after the bite." Malc's flat tone did not convey sympathy. It did not convey anything but fact.

"She didn't happen to be white, did she?"

"No."

"What happened to the twins?"

"There is no record of them."

"Is there anything about their father?"

"No."

"Where did she live?"

"Unknown."

Luke said, "Her parents should have had another child."

"Rachel Toback is her younger sister."

"So, if the twins survived surgery, they could be with their father or Rachel, maybe."

"Speculation."

"Yeah. You're right. Forget it. It's probably got nothing to do with the case anyway. What else have you got for me?"

"The World Church of Eternal Vision is a small, illegal organization with groups in London, Bristol, Manchester, and Edinburgh. Its members call themselves Visionaries. Their numbers are uncertain but few. Little is known about them, but they believe in a mystical supreme creator called God."

"A creator who is brown," Luke added.

"Of course. Any other color is deemed wicked."

"Charming. Where do they hang out?"

Malc hesitated. "I have no record of them hanging out."

"I mean, where do they meet?"

"They move premises at regular intervals to avoid detection. Each new address is kept secret."

"Thinking of meetings," Luke said, "does London's white community get together? Do they have meetings? If they do, I want to be at the next one. Owen Goode might be there."

"Searching."

"Have you got anything on crimes against whites yet?"

"I have extracted data from all of London's mobile aids to law and crime where a victim was stated to be white. There may be other cases where skin color was not specified. There is no evidence for systematic murder or assault on the basis of skin color. The last casualty reported to be white skinned was murdered 14 months ago. However, there is a pattern of property damage, mostly arson. There may be a campaign to drive whites out of some neighborhoods in London."

"Interesting. Store that information, Malc, even though it doesn't get me closer to Owen Goode."

"There is no accessible data on meetings of the white community."

"That's a shame."

Malc said, "I have received an order for an immediate virtual meeting with the Pairing Committee. Sending video to the telescreen."

Luke glanced at his watch and muttered, "Right on time." At once, he sat up as straight as if he was on trial.

Chapter Nine

The telescreen came to life with a panel of four people. Like the pairing process itself, they were very carefully balanced. Sitting behind a long table, the two women were aged around 30 and 60, and the two men were roughly 40 and 50 years old. The older woman, the head of the committee, got to her feet. First she introduced herself as Shetal Darke and then named the others on the panel.

Shetal smiled. "I think I can call you Luke. Yes?"

Luke nodded. "Sure."

"I should welcome you to London. You'll find it different from Birmingham. Still, I hope you'll enjoy your stay and, of course, help us out."

"Thanks." Luke waited nervously for the real purpose of this linkup. He waited for bad news.

The image occupied most of one wall of the room, so it seemed like the committee's chamber had been bolted onto his living quarters. Luke felt like he could reach out and touch the members.

Shetal glanced down at her notes. "I have the plans made by the Birmingham Pairing Committee before it was overtaken by unfortunate events concerning your last case. We have examined the policy in some detail and agree that Georgia Bowie, currently a biologist in

Dundee, is an ideal match for you, Luke. We cannot see any good reason for changing these arrangements. When The Time comes, you will be paired with Georgia. This committee will now ratify . . . ”

Luke did not have the time to be dismayed by the decision before he was overwhelmed by horror.

First all four members of the Pairing Committee looked to the right at the same time. Of course, Luke could not see what had distracted them. All that he could see was their reaction. Shetal's mouth opened in shock, but no words emerged. The younger man threw himself under the table, but the older one froze in terror. The other woman put her hand over her mouth. From behind her palm, she let out a stifled cry. “No! Please. No.”

To Luke—watching from afar, yet seeing it up close—everything seemed to happen in slow motion.

There was the muffled noise of a shotgun blast. A sudden spray of red blossomed behind Shetal as the impact of the bullet in her chest knocked her violently backward.

The younger woman's hand still covered her mouth as she turned in her seat toward Shetal. Her shriek was louder this time. “No!” The second shot thudded into her shoulder with a horrible splintering sound. She screamed as she fell to the floor.

Luke heard the third shot, but the reaction to it was

not so dramatic. Under the table, the younger man had curled himself up into a ball, arms wrapped protectively around his head. He jolted and then slowly toppled over like a snail that had lost its grip on the ground.

Alone, the old man sat at the table, still staring through his glasses at the person beyond Luke's view. He was mesmerized. His expression had gone beyond fear. He was petrified, completely unable to move. But he knew that he was next.

Luke felt like he was a part of the massacre because he seemed to be sharing the same room. But he was a distant bystander. He could not stop it. He could not rush in and help. Around a mile away, he could not even tell Malc to follow the assassin. He could only watch helplessly.

Malc had already alerted The Authorities, but it would be minutes before guards could get to the scene. That would be too late.

Realizing that the last committee member must be looking straight down the barrel of a gun, Luke winced. Holding his breath, Luke prepared himself for the awful sight of a bullet cracking a skull, but oddly it didn't happen. There was complete silence instead of another explosion.

The man's expression did not change. With eyes fixed on the same spot, he sat and sat, and nothing happened.

Then, at last, three people ran into the chamber. A

noisy chaos replaced the eerie quiet. The picture on Luke's telescreen broke up and abruptly disappeared.

For the first time Luke had seen a murder played out live in front of him, and he felt completely sick. For a minute, he could not speak.

When he next heard a voice, he said, "What? Excuse me?"

"Are you all right, Luke?" Malc asked. "Do you need assistance?"

"No. I'm . . . okay." He took some deep breaths to calm himself. He felt that he should be doing something, but he was detached from it all. It was not even his case. Even so, he could not stop his training from kicking in. He was an investigator by instinct. "Malc, those pictures and sounds, is there any way you can keep them?"

"Not completely. As soon as I realized that a crime was taking place, I started to record."

"What have you got? Show me."

Malc's recording began as soon as the second victim cried "No!" and the gun fired.

Choked, Luke sat through it all again. "Can you analyze the soundtrack? What type of weapon makes that exact noise? Can you distinguish different ones?"

"In theory, that should be possible because different types of firearms have different interior ballistics. The hammer or firing pin strikes the primer cup and explodes a chemical mixture. The shower of hot particles penetrates and ignites the propellant. This produces a large volume of hot gas that forces the bullet out of the barrel. All firearms function in this way, but the three steps are distinctive to each type. However, I do not have a database of discharge sounds. I could request the information, but the investigator assigned to the case will simply examine the spent bullets and cartridge cases to get better information."

"All right. Do a detailed search of any noises apart from the second victim's shout and the gunshots. Did the person with the gun say anything? Amplify, and play me anything interesting."

"There is evidence of human speech after the second shot. However, it is short, quiet, and incomplete."

As the gunshot echoed and faded, there was the end of an utterance, mixed with the ghastly noise of disintegrating bone and a scream. The fragment of speech sounded like " . . . ect."

Luke listened to it five times and was none the wiser. It could have been the end of a word like "wrecked." "Can you enhance it, Malc? How about taking the tail end of the third gunshot and subtracting it from the second? Will I get to hear the rest?"

Once Malc had processed the sound Luke listened again and thought that he heard another consonant. Now the voice seemed to be saying "pecked." Luke shrugged. "I don't know. Is it a male or a female voice? I can't even tell that."

"Uncertain."

"Okay. Send it to Jade. Ask her if she can analyze that voice. What does it say, and is it a man, woman, boy, or girl? Right now I want to try something with the pictures instead. Give me a close-up of the old man's glasses."

Squinting, Luke concentrated on the blurry image on both lenses. "There! Stop. Give me the last few seconds again. What's that?"

"It is a reflection of movement."

"Exactly. Isn't it someone spinning around by the door and walking out?"

"That is possible," Malc replied. "However . . ."

"I know it's not going to identify anyone," Luke said. "But it's someone in a big coat. The head looks a little peculiar. Maybe it's some kind of hat or hood. Anyway, if the FI in charge analyzes the shape against the size of the door frame, it'd give us a good idea of height."

Malc paused and then said, "That is a novel use of technology, and it is likely to give useful data."

Beginning to recover from the shock of witnessing three shootings, Luke said, "You almost sound impressed. I'll take that as a compliment."

"I remind you that this is not your case."

"No. Forward the idea to The Authorities.

It might help the investigator."

"Processing and transmitting."

The telescreen flickered back into life. This time it was a larger-than-life image of the hotel chef. "Investigator Harding. Sorry to interrupt. A messenger's just delivered an emergency supply of pomegranates from Birmingham. But they're marked 'For Forensic Use Only'."

"That's all right," Luke replied with a smile. "It means only forensic investigators get to eat them."

The chef returned the grin. "Of course. Leave it to me."

"Thanks."

"Are you all right? You don't look well."

"I'm fine, thanks. But before you go," Luke said, "do you employ anyone in the hotel who's white, by any chance?"

"Uh, yes, we do."

"Who's that?"

"Elodie. One of our maids."

"Is she in the hotel right now?"

"I think so. Should I get someone to send her up to you?"

Luke didn't want to scare her with a summons to see an investigator. "No. Just tell me where she is."

"I don't know. Reception will be able to help though. I'll put you through to Mr. Morgan. Just a moment."

The telescreen went to standby mode for two minutes before a receptionist appeared. "I'm sorry," she said, "Mr. Morgan is feeling sick and has gone to see his doctor. But the chef tells me you want to know where Elodie is. She's on the third floor, preparing rooms."

"Thanks. I'll find her."

Luke soon located Elodie making a bed. Being an albino, she was easy to spot. Except for her eyes and lips, everything about her was pale. Her skin was milky, and her hair was white. Even her eyebrows were colorless. Set in that ashen face, her lips seemed bright red, and her eyes had conspicuous pink pupils.

"Meetings?" she said in answer to his question about London's white community. "Yes. As it happens, there's one tonight."

At once, Luke perked up. "Where? And what time?"

"Clement School. 7:30."

"Thanks," Luke replied. "I'll be there."

Chapter Ten

With his large bald head poking out of a waterproof coat, the intimidating guard standing at the entrance of the school looked with disapproval at Luke. "You're not white," he stated.

"Nice going," Luke said to him with a playful grin. "But I am invited. I'm meeting Owen Goode—who is white. Do you know him?"

The looming bouncer shook his head. "They just use me to keep out trouble. I don't know most of them." He held the door open for Luke and Malc.

Luke got the impression that the guard would have checked him out much more thoroughly if he hadn't been a forensic investigator. Walking into the reception area and looking through the doorway into the brightly lit room, Luke was appalled. Clement School was nothing like Birmingham School. The building was very shabby. In places paint was peeling off the walls, wood looked rotten, and windows were cracked. Two buckets had been placed carefully to catch drops from the leaking roof.

When he walked into the assembly room, the buzz of conversation died down for a few seconds as the gathering people turned and gazed at him. Luke was not worried. He could tell that they were curious about him rather than hostile. Ignoring their reaction, he looked around, trying to spot a 15-year-old boy with a bandage on his left hand.

Within seconds, a middle-aged woman approached him and said, “This isn’t an illegal meeting, you know.”

“I know. I’m here to catch up with a friend of mine. Owen Goode. Is he here, do you know?”

“Owen? He shows up sometimes. He’s a little unpredictable, to tell you the truth. He hasn’t done anything wrong, has he?”

Luke smiled. “No. I just want to talk to him.”

The woman looked unconvinced.

Luke turned to Malc and said, “Is Owen Goode under any kind of suspicion?”

“No,” the mobile answered.

Reassured, the woman relaxed. “You’re welcome, FI . . .”

“Luke Harding. And you are . . .?”

“Cleo McGrath. I’m leading the meeting. You might find one or two items interesting. We’re going to discuss crimes against whites, for one thing.”

Luke nodded. “Good. Is that why you’ve got a bouncer at the door?”

Cleo nodded. “It’s sad. We never used to but . . .” She shrugged. “We don’t have a choice these days.”

“Is it personal attacks or damage to homes?”

She seemed surprised that Luke was aware of the

problem. "Are you here to investigate it?" she said eagerly.

"Not really," Luke replied. "But I'm not sure what I am investigating until I talk to Owen, so maybe I am."

Cleo was smiling broadly. "That would be great. The Authorities have never taken us seriously before. I thought they didn't believe us."

To Malc, Luke said, "Repeat your findings on crimes against whites."

"There is no evidence of assault or murder in which the motive is skin color. However, there may be a campaign to drive whites out of some neighborhoods in London through property damage, mostly arson."

Cleo was almost gleeful now. "That's it exactly! You are taking us seriously. Wait until I tell the others. You really *are* welcome."

Just before she took off toward the stage, Luke said, "You will point out Owen if he shows up, won't you?"

"Of course."

When Cleo began her speech, Luke noticed Elodie from the Central Hotel standing to the left of the stage. By the time that Cleo got around to the topic of crime and told the crowd that a forensic investigator was looking into their complaints, Luke spotted a white boy entering the hall. He was shorter than Luke but just as wiry and in good shape. And he had a bandage on his left hand.

On the stage Cleo hesitated. "Ah, Owen," she said.

"Thanks for coming. Late as ever."

The boy looked surprised that he'd been singled out and greeted, but Luke knew why Cleo had announced Owen's arrival. Luke detached himself from the back of the crowd and headed for the newcomer.

Almost immediately, Malc said to him very quietly, "I am sensing traces of accelerant and products of combustion in the air."

At once, Luke halted. "You mean, there's a fire?" he whispered.

"Correct."

"I can't smell it yet. Where's it coming from?"

Malc moved a few feet away and completed a circle around Luke. "The signal is strongest toward the back of the school, behind the stage."

Immediately, Luke changed his priorities. He was very eager to speak to Owen Goode, but if someone was attempting to murder an entire group of whites, the interview with Owen would have to wait. Pushing his way to the raised stage, he looked around for an exit. Beyond Elodie, there was a door. Before he dashed toward it he interrupted Cleo. "Get everyone out at the front. I think there's a problem."

With Malc behind him, Luke opened the back door carefully. It led into a darkened storeroom stacked with old chairs, overhead projectors, whiteboards, and flip charts. Luke sniffed the air and, for the first time, smelled smoke. He weaved his way through the stacks of equipment to the only other door and placed his flat palm against it. The surface wasn't warm, so he didn't expect the fire to be right on the other side. Edging out of the storeroom, he found himself in a short corridor with a coatroom. The whole area was choked with gray fumes. The windows across from him had been smashed. Paper and a lot of other garbage had been pushed through the holes, soaked with flammable liquid, and set on fire. The air was thick with the smell of fuel and burning. The inside wall next to the window was on fire, and black smoke was gathering at the ceiling like an angry storm cloud. The open windows provided fresh oxygen to feed the flames.

Luke coughed and then slammed the door shut on the blaze. "Have you notified The Authorities?" he asked Malc.

"Confirmed."

"There's a radiator in the corner. If you hit a weak spot with your laser, can you drill a hole?"

"Confirmed. But it will be very narrow."

"So you can't make enough water spurt out to put out the fire?" Luke coughed again, clearing his lungs of the acrid air.

"No."

"Okay. I give up. We're out of here. If the building's clear, at least no one's going to get hurt."

"The fire's progress is likely to be slow and limited because the building is damp," Malc said as they retraced their steps through the storeroom, "but the atmosphere will soon be poisonous to humans."

The room was deserted. The air inside it had become a faint blue haze. While Luke held his breath, kept his head down, and sprinted through it, Malc said, "There is a second source of combustion on the other side of the premises."

Luke burst through the main doors, out into the fresh air, coughed, and then looked for Cleo by the light of the lamps. She was standing with the guard, watching smoke emerge from both sides of the building. "Is everyone out?" asked Luke.

"Yes. Are you all right?"

"Fine. Where's Owen?"

They all looked around.

When Owen saw them staring at him, he jumped, turned, and darted north along Drury Corridor.

Luke sighed and took off after him. He did not doubt for a moment that he could keep up with Owen, but seeing how quickly the white boy could run, he had to admit that he might not be able to overtake him. Knowing also that Owen would be much more familiar with London, he suspected that the boy might be able to lose him in the maze of walkways and alleys. He said to Malc, "Go after him. Don't harm him, though. Obstruct mode only."

Chapter Eleven

Over the years Owen had learned to be suspicious of almost everyone. Londoners with weapons in their hands or The Authorities and their investigators were all the same to him. They were best avoided.

The forensic investigator's mobile flew past him, halted, and then came straight at him. Owen swore under his breath and dived to one side to avoid colliding with the machine. Even before he'd recovered from the stumble, the robot was zooming toward his head. He ducked, lost his footing, and staggered before he regained his balance and speed.

Just as he was about to turn left on to Long Acre, a faint red beam came out of the mobile, directed at the ground in front of him. A weed sizzled and died as soon as the laser beam zapped it. Owen gulped but ignored the demonstration. After all, it was only a warning shot. He gambled on the fact that the machine wouldn't attack him.

On Long Acre he skirted around a leafless ash tree growing in the middle of the corridor and came face-to-face with the mobile again. This time he tripped over a rusty fallen sign and fell onto a bush.

It was hopeless. He had planned to lose the investigator in the zigzags of Covent Garden, but this robot was going to follow him everywhere. He threw up his hands in frustration.

Ignoring the stinging sensation in his smoky lungs, Luke veered on to Long Acre and sprinted up to Owen. The boy was flat on the ground, with Malc hovering threateningly above him.

Smiling, Luke held out his hand. "You're a pretty good runner. If you weren't so fast, I wouldn't have set Malc on you. Sorry about that. I only want to talk. You're not in trouble."

Giving up, Owen got to his feet without taking Luke's hand. "Always in trouble."

"Not from me. I just want to ask you about that." He pointed toward Owen's bandage.

Owen glanced at his left hand and frowned. "I got shot. That's all."

"Where?"

"Where does it look like? In the hand."

"No," Luke said. "I mean, where in London."

"Oh. Tottenham Court Corridor. Just above Oxford Freeway."

"Who shot you?"

Owen shrugged.

"Didn't you see?"

"No," Owen answered.

"Did anyone follow you to the hospital?"

"Not that I saw."

Disturbed by the two boys, a tree snake slithered along a branch of the ash tree and out of their range.

"How did you get along with the doctor at Thomas's Hospital?" asked Luke.

"Didn't know what to think of her at first. Think she thought I was a little dangerous. She wanted an identity card. But she did the job all right."

"Do you know why you were shot?"

"Think so."

"Oh?"

Owen sighed. "Someone shouted, 'White scum!'"

"Mmm," Luke muttered sadly. He did not express his disapproval because he didn't want to interrupt the flow of answers. "Male or female?"

"Couldn't tell. Didn't hang around to find out."

"Can you take me to the place? I could use some spent bullets."

Head bowed, Owen muttered, "You stopped us from getting hurt in the school, didn't you?"

"So it seems."

"Guess I owe you. But I don't have to take you anywhere."

"Why's that?"

When Owen pulled out a penknife from his pocket, Malc moved closer to protect Luke, but Luke did not flinch. He'd already decided that the boy was harmless.

Owen bent down and used the penknife to flick a chunk of metal out of the rubber of his sole. Standing up again, he let the bullet drop into Luke's open palm.

Luke beamed. "Thanks. That's fantastic. And amazing. You were lucky. A couple of inches higher, and you wouldn't have been running anywhere."

"Why do you want it?"

"You don't want people shooting you on the walkways, do you?"

"What's that got to do with it?"

"I'm on a case—someone at Thomas's Hospital was shot soon after you left. It could be the same rifle. I need to check out the bullet."

"You're lucky too. Lucky I left it in my shoe."

"Yeah. Have you got anything else for me?"

"Maybe."

"What?" Luke asked.

"An address on a piece of paper."

Luke frowned. "Does it have anything to do with you getting shot?"

Owen shrugged, hesitated, and then changed his mind. "Sure it does. What are you offering for it?"

It was clear to Luke that Owen was on a mission. He was better at spotting a business opportunity than a significant clue. "I'll offer to stop Malc from drilling a second hole in your hand with his laser."

Owen paused, unsure of himself, and then said,

"You're kidding me. That's against the law. Isn't it?"

Malc interrupted. "Confirmed."

"All right," Luke said with a wry smile. "Give me the address—just in case it's important—and I won't have you arrested for withholding evidence. How's that for a deal? It's the best you'll get."

Owen shuffled from foot to foot for a few seconds before caving in. He fished around in his pockets until he found the strip of paper and then handed it to Luke.

By lamplight, it looked like a page from a small notepad. Someone had written "72 Russell Plaza" on it in blue ink. Luke knew it was useless to ask Malc to scan the message or to analyze the handwriting or the ink because Owen had interfered with it, and it could never be linked for sure with any crime. "Where did you get it?"

"On Tottenham Court. Blew into me just before the firing started. Maybe it's another reason I got shot. I don't know."

"Where did it come from?"

"Didn't really see. I was more interested in getting away."

Luke slipped it into his own pocket. "Thanks. I'll look into it. Anything else you can tell me? Anything at all?"

Owen shook his head, but then he had second thoughts. "How old are you? Sixteen, 17?"

"16."

"Young for an investigator."

"So?" Luke prompted.

"You're the same as me, really. Around the same age, both by ourselves in London. I've helped you. You should help me now."

"I thought we were friends already. What do you want?"

Owen smiled for the first time. "A clean identity card."

Luke nodded. "I can't promise you. And anyway, how would I get it to you?"

Owen thought for a moment. "Cleo McGrath's all right, I guess. I'll keep in touch with her. She's got an address, a card, and all. You can find me through her."

"Okay. I'll see what I can do. And I'll tell The Authorities you were helpful."

"Can I go?"

Luke nodded. "Take care."

Owen walked a few paces but then stopped and turned back. "You're a pretty good runner yourself," he said, "but you cheated."

Luke grinned at him. "Yeah. I'm known for that. But I prefer to call it using all the tools available to me."

Back at Clement School firefighters had put out the flames and obliterated any traces of the person who had tried to make an inferno of the place—and the white community inside. Some of them still lingered outside, unable to take in what had almost happened.

Seeing Luke return, Cleo went up to him right away. "Now will you investigate?" she said, waving a hand toward the smoldering school.

"I don't know. I need to follow up on a couple of things Owen's given me. But if there's a link with my own case, yes, I'll do it."

Cleo almost jumped on him in her enthusiasm. "Good. After all, this wasn't arson. It was attempted mass murder."

Malc replied, "That would be the case only if the arsonist acted deliberately, knowing that there were people inside."

Cleo ignored Malc. Talking to Luke, she said, "Do you doubt for one second that whoever set it on fire knew we were inside?"

"It fits the pattern," Luke replied. He walked away, saying, "I'll get back to you."

Chapter Twelve

In the makeshift laboratory of his hotel room Luke placed Owen's bullet on a small set of scales in order to record its weight. He stood it on its base so that Malc could measure its precise dimensions and scan its markings.

Malc reported, "This is a nine-millimeter-caliber bullet, rifled with six grooves, inclined to the right."

"Has anyone else reported the same rifling marks on any other bullets?"

"Processing."

Luke jolted in surprise when a branch, bent by the wind, slapped against his window while the rain continued its steady drumming on the glass.

"Today," Malc announced, "identical marks were found on a bullet of the same caliber recovered from the chamber of the London Pairing Committee."

"What?" Luke cried.

"Identical striations were . . ."

"Yes," said Luke. "I heard. I'm just . . . taking it in. You said a bullet. But there were three shots, not one."

"It was the bullet that killed Shetal Darke. It passed right through her body. The second and third bullets have not yet been extracted from the bodies of the other two victims."

"So whoever fired at Owen Goode gunned down the Pairing Committee."

"That is likely but not confirmed. It is possible to conclude only that the bullets were discharged from the same rifle barrel."

"And Anna Suleman may well have been shot with a nine-millimeter-caliber rifle."

"Correct. However, without the bullet, there is no proven link to her murder."

Luke nodded. "I know. I'm solving every case but my own."

"That is an exaggeration," Malc said in his emotionless voice.

"First thing tomorrow—after I've tested one of those pomegranates—we're going to 72 Russell Plaza. Who knows whose case I might solve there?"

Malc's mention of pairing reminded Luke that he needed to talk to Jade. To prepare himself, he went to his bedroom and lay down in the dark. "Malc, the usual image on the ceiling, please. And give me Jade's latest chill-out music, volume 12."

For ten minutes Luke let her soothing electronic melody wash over him as he watched the stars in the virtual sky that Malc projected onto the ceiling. Then he said, "That's better. Fade to volume two and connect me to Jade, please. Speech only." This time he couldn't bear to show himself or to see her face.

Her voice boomed over the music, “Hi there, Harding!”

“Hi. I’m just listening to your stuff. What can I say?”

“You could say ‘perfect,’ ‘genius,’ or just plain old ‘brilliant’ if you’re feeling critical.”

“It’s all of those.”

“You sound a little grumpy,” Jade said. “Do you get pomegranate breakfasts down there?”

“Yes and no. The hotel was a little surprised. Never had an order for them before . . .”

Jade interrupted with a giggle. “Proof the place is primitive.”

“Eating them’s a minority sport. Anyway, it’s okay because I’m getting them shipped down from Birmingham.”

“Anything to keep a top forensic investigator happy, huh?”

“That’s one advantage of the job,” Luke replied. “I might as well milk it.”

Bluntly, Jade asked, “What’s wrong?”

“What do you mean?”

“Come on,” she said. “I don’t have to be in the same room to hear an edge in your voice.”

“Your ears are just too good.” Luke paused and then said, “Did you get that sound recording I sent?”

“You want me to do your job as well as mine now, huh? Anyway, I’m still working on it. It’s tricky. The

noise of the gun going off covers up just about everything else, but I haven't given up. I'll tell you if I get anything."

"Thanks. It'd really help."

"That wasn't what you were calling about."

"No," Luke admitted. "It's the Pairing Committee result." There was a sudden silence from Sheffield. "They agreed with Birmingham about Georgia."

Jade sighed. After a few seconds she said, "It's not exactly a shock, is it? Even so . . ."

Making them both jump, Malc butted in to their conversation. "Strictly, the Pairing Committee was not able to ratify the arrangement, so it is not yet official."

"Why not?" asked Jade, grateful yet puzzled.

"It sounds like a fantasy," Luke answered, "but someone burst in and shot three of them."

"What?"

"You're working on the case. That's where the sound came from."

Shocked, she repeated, "What?"

"I know. It's crazy, but that's what happened." Trying to lighten the mood, he added, "And it wasn't me."

"You said London's got its good points. From up here, they're not obvious."

"What about you? When does the Sheffield committee meet?"

"I don't know exactly, but it won't be long. Let's face

it, there won't be good news either." Jade paused before adding, "But I doubt if they'll be gunned down."

A dense layer of gray clouds was lumbering across the morning sky when Luke unlocked 72 Russell Plaza with his identity card. He pushed the rickety door open slowly, not knowing if anyone lived there. But as soon as he peered inside, he realized that the place had been abandoned. It smelled damp, and the only pieces of furniture in the main room were four long wooden benches. Staying in the doorway, Luke could see that the window looked out on a small cluttered park that had become wild. Inside, the wall to the left of the window was cracked from the floorboards to the ceiling.

Luke did not contaminate the scene by entering. "Malc, go in and scan everything." While the mobile went about his work Luke closed his eyes and breathed in deeply through his nose. Behind the mustiness, there was something familiar. "Analyze the air. What do you smell?"

"There are several odor-producing chemicals."

"I think there's something I've come across before on this case."

"You may be detecting traces of diallyl disulfide. It is highly pungent."

"Garlic again. Like on the autobarge."

"Correct."

With his tongue, Luke yanked a pomegranate seed out from between two of his teeth and swallowed it. Hearing excited cries behind him, Luke turned and watched three boys chasing a fox across the collapsing freeway. Concentrating on the room again, he examined it for a few minutes while Malc continued to sweep across it, recording everything. "What's that in the corner? Piles of paper?"

"There are two different pamphlets," Malc answered. "You already have a copy of one that denounces whites. The second condemns the pairing process."

"Interesting," Luke muttered to himself. "So this must be where the Visionaries met. That fits." He hesitated before adding, "They don't like whites, and Owen was shot. They don't like pairing, and the London Pairing Committee was massacred. Then there's Anna Suleman. Makes you wonder what they think about doctors."

"I have collected some fragments of skin from the area in front of the bench."

"Skin?"

"Testing. It is nonhuman."

"Have you recorded all of it now?"

"Confirmed."

"Good." Luke slipped on a pair of gloves and walked into the room for the first time. He went straight to the stacks of leaflets, but before he took a copy of each, he hesitated. One of the pamphlets on the top was wrinkled as if it had got wet. Curious, he looked up but saw no sign of water seeping from the ceiling or walls. "Malc, what's been on this leaflet?"

"Unknown. But there is a trace deposit of DNA. Saliva is a possibility."

Luke frowned. "Someone's drooled on it? Weird. Unless it was a baby, I guess. Can you get a DNA fingerprint?"

"Not here. I need to amplify the traces in a laboratory first."

Waiting for Malc to complete his tests on the fragments of skin, Luke put the crinkly paper into an evidence bag and then read the second pamphlet. There were some ideas—criminal ideas—that caught Luke's eye. Visionaries believed that the choice of a partner should have everything to do with love and nothing to do with absurd committees.

Luke glanced at Malc and said, "You're taking a long time."

"There are samples of skin from two nonhuman species. I am attempting to identify both."

"Two? They were running an animal sanctuary in here?"

"Unlikely," Malc replied.

Getting down on his hands and knees, Luke remarked, "There are some hairs, too."

"Seventy-two detected. Some appear to be identical,

so they are not from 72 different individuals, but they are all human and female."

"No men's?" Luke paused, thinking. "Those two boys who gave me the leaflet had shaved heads. Maybe male Visionaries cut off all of their hair for some reason. That's a convenient belief if they're doing something illegal—and a nuisance for an FI."

"The two skin types are from a rattlesnake and a sheep," Malc announced.

Luke grimaced. "That's a funny combination."

"I am not equipped to understand humor."

"You're not so good with language either," Luke retorted. "People feed snakes rats, squirrels, and rabbits. They'd be pushing their luck to get one to swallow a sheep." His mind went back to the contents of the autobarge, and he asked, "Is there anything else that says sheep have been in here, like droppings or grass or something?"

"No."

"How about woolen fibers?"

"Yet to be confirmed, but there appear to be several."

Luke grinned. "Woolen fibers and skin but no other signs of sheep. Sounds like someone in a sheepskin coat to me. Maybe one stolen from the barge by a garlic-loving bandit."

"Speculation."

"Look," Luke said, making up his mind about what to

do, "you could be analyzing things in here all day . . ."

"It will take four hours and 11 minutes more, approximately."

"Yeah. And I want you working on the DNA from this leaflet. So call in The Authorities to bag it all up, deliver it to my quarters, and seal the room in case I want to come back. After all, it might not have anything to do with Anna Suleman, and we're just wasting time."

It took Malc three hours to isolate and replicate the dried DNA from the leaflet, but it was worth the effort. "I have a DNA profile," he reported to Luke eventually.

"Run a comparison with London's database. If there's no match, use the criminal collections."

Several minutes later Malc said, "No match."

Luke sighed. Then, in a moment of inspiration, he said, "Log on to Thomas's Hospital again then. Check it against their medical files."

It took only seconds this time. "There is an almost perfect match with two patients."

"Two patients?" Luke sat up to attention. "But that's not possible. Everyone's got a unique . . ." He stopped and smiled broadly. "The twins. The Toback boys. They'll have identical DNA."

"Correct," Malc replied.

It was for moments like these that Luke was a forensic investigator. He was almost shivering with pleasure. At last he could see a link. Dr. Anna Suleman—the first victim—had operated on the Toback twins at Thomas's Hospital. The Toback family seemed to be part of The World Church of Eternal Vision, whose members hated Pairing Committees and white people. And Luke suspected that an out-of-control Visionary had slaughtered most of the London Pairing Committee and attempted to murder the white Owen Goode.

"You got information about Rachel Toback yesterday," Luke said to Malc. "Did it include her address?" He held his breath.

"Confirmed."

Luke grinned. "Great! Grab your coat, Malc. We're off."

"I do not have or require a coat."

Chapter Thirteen

Just north of Euston Plaza, Cranleigh Walkway was crammed with weeds, bushes, and trees. At one end crumbling buildings had long since lost their roofs. They were home only to bats, rats, and foxes. Yet, at the other end, the tall duplex houses were in good shape. Rachel Toback occupied a small, clean, and comfortable set of rooms on the top floor. She was 17, very thin, and timid. She wasn't wearing makeup, her hair was tangled, and her clothes were plain.

Luke introduced himself and sat down in the seat that Rachel offered him.

"What's this about?" Rachel said, tension written all over her face.

Luke took out the two pamphlets from the pocket of his coat. "Do you recognize these?"

"Yes."

"They're put out by The World Church of Eternal Vision," Luke said, reading from the small print. "Do you know anything about it? I think you do."

"Why do you ask?"

"Because I read them, and well, they're so right," said Luke, faking it convincingly. "Especially the part about Pairing Committees."

Rachel looked at him suspiciously.

Expecting her to be aware that mobile aids to law and crime could not lie, Luke turned toward Malc and asked, "Am I known to be dissatisfied with Pairing Committees?"

"Confirmed."

Less tense, Rachel asked, "How did you find me?"

Luke almost stuck with the truth. "Someone told me where the Church met. I went to Russell Plaza, found a few biological samples, and, after some forensic analysis, your name cropped up. So, here I am. That's a perk of being an investigator." He looked around the uncluttered room and, seeing a stroller and toys, smiled and said, "You've got a baby. You're young for that."

Rachel became jittery again and did not reply.

"Just an observation," Luke said. "Don't worry. I'm not chasing unlicensed children—or members of the Church. Malc, am I under instruction to investigate Visionaries or unauthorized births?"

"No."

Rachel said, "The kids aren't mine."

"More than one?"

"Twins."

Luke nodded. "Ah. Of course. They must be your sister's. Sarah, wasn't it?"

"How do you know that?"

"When your name came up on the system, it gave me a file on you. How are the twins? Okay now?"

She waved toward one of the doors. "Fine. Asleep, for the moment."

"I'm sorry about Sarah. What happened to her?"

"I don't know," Rachel answered, shuffling uncomfortably in her chair. "They said she'd been bitten by a snake."

Luke was surprised that she didn't seem more upset. "She didn't manage to get to the hospital."

Rachel pulled back as if the thought of a hospital filled her with dread.

Luke noted her reaction and decided to change his angle of attack. "You've got a nice place here."

"Visionaries are very caring. They look after me and the boys. That's why I've got this apartment."

"What do you think of Thomas's Hospital? The twins would've had a different life if they hadn't been separated."

Rachel hesitated and then said, "God wanted them to live as one, to wear the same skin. Sarah should've respected that."

Luke sat on the edge of his seat. "You know, that's exactly what I think." He was getting the impression that Visionaries did not approve of the medical profession. Encouraging her to say more, he shook his head and muttered, "Doctors."

"We don't have the right to interfere. No one does. But doctors meddle with God's good work all

of the time."

"I know what you mean," Luke replied enthusiastically. "My father was a doctor, and when my kid sister got sick, he couldn't help her. She died when she was a baby." To convince her that he shared her views, he invented something on the spot. "The only time I went to a doctor—I had a cyst—she didn't help. Not at all. It just got worse and worse until I changed my lifestyle. Then it cleared up all on its own."

"Amen."

Luke nodded. "But there's something I don't understand. If, like me, you don't trust doctors, why did Sarah take the twins to the hospital?"

Rachel sighed heavily. "I guess she broke the faith to make her life easier. Or theirs. I don't know. But I was . . . ashamed."

"Who's the father? Is he a Visionary? What did he think about it?"

"Samuel. He . . . I don't know. He said Sarah did the wrong thing. But I didn't see him stopping her from going to the hospital."

Luke thought that Rachel would see through him if he asked for Samuel's full name. He decided to take a different route. "He must visit you—to spend time with his children."

Rachel nodded. "When he can, yes."

Luke leaned even closer to her, like they were

exchanging secrets. "You know, I'd love to come to one of your meetings. I think it'd be perfect for me."

Rachel looked doubtful, glancing up at Malc. "I'd have to ask Ethan."

"Ethan?"

"Ethan Loach. He's our preacher."

Luke stood up and shrugged casually. "Fine. I'd be happy to meet him—anywhere he likes. He's bound to be worried about me because I'm an investigator. I understand. But I think I'll be able to persuade him that I'm genuine. I can tell him exactly why I hate pairing. Either of you can send me a telescreen message, letting me know when and where. No problem." He handed her a card that gave his electronic address. "If I don't hear from you, I'll come back in a few days. Okay?" Before he went to the door he said, "It's been great talking to you. Thanks. You've really cheered me up."

"Respect," Rachel said.

Luke hesitated. "Respect?" he murmured thoughtfully. Then he grinned and replied, "Yeah. Respect."

Standing by a streaming window in his hotel suite, Luke said, "This rain! It takes forever to arrive, and then it doesn't stop."

"Illogical and impossible," Malc replied.

Luke ignored his mobile. "Time for a summary.

It won't take long. The World Church of Eternal Vision doesn't like whites, pairing, or doctors. It would despise Owen Goode, the London Pairing Committee, Dr. Anna Suleman, and Sarah Toback—because she went to a doctor to save her twins. And most of them are dead. The ones that aren't dead have been attacked. I think I know where to look for Lost Bullet."

"There was no evidence to suggest that Sarah Toback was murdered," Malc replied.

"No, but she was bitten by a snake, and you found rattlesnake skin where the Visionaries met."

"That is an appropriate but unconvincing observation."

"Go through the crime statistics again, Malc. Look for raids on Pairing Committee chambers, doctors' offices, and hospitals." Luke turned back to the window to watch the latest downpour while Malc searched the databases.

"Three Pairing Committee premises in outer London have been firebombed in the last six months. Fifteen doctors' offices and hospitals in the city have reported some degree of vandalism."

Luke nodded. "Whites, Pairing Committees, and doctors. What we're seeing is not so much murder as tribal cleansing. Present it all to The Authorities, Malc. The Suleman case has suddenly got much bigger. Tomorrow morning I want to be the FI in charge of the assassination of the London Pairing Committee and the attempted murder of Owen Goode and a lot of other white people. And while I'm waiting, get me everything you can find on Ethan Loach."

Chapter Fourteen

"Call me a genius," said Jade with a huge grin on her face.

Luke looked at the time written on the telescreen. It was almost midnight. As soon as he saw Jade's image, though, he didn't feel drowsy. "I'm always calling you a genius. And you've got superb ears—better than Malc's. What have you got for me?"

"A word."

"What word?"

"You just want an answer, don't you? You don't want to hear my imaginative solution and how I subtracted each frequency . . ."

"You're right," Luke replied. "I'm sure you did it beautifully, and I bet no one else could have done it."

"I really should explain such a fantastic technical achievement—it'd be good for your education and sense of wonder—but I'll just say 'respect'."

"Respect?"

"That's the word behind the gunshot, the scream, and the awful sound of shattering bone."

"Are you sure?" asked Luke.

"Certain."

"Thanks, Jade. You're a miracle worker. But . . . uh . . . was it a male or female voice?"

Jade laughed. "Not that much of a miracle worker. By the time I'd finished with it, it was almost completely distorted. If I had to guess, I'd say it was a man, but you'd struggle to recognize it as human at all.

Outside the Pairing Committee's chamber there were three bunches of lilies. Inside it felt to Luke like he was in the enemy's camp. This was the room where he would be denied a life with Jade Vernon. It was also where Lost Bullet had stood two days ago. The table, the floor underneath, and the wall behind were still stained brown with blood. "So," Luke said, "Lost Bullet came through that door and stopped here. Exactly here. And yet he—or she—didn't leave a single fiber or hair or footprint, even though it was wet outside."

"Correct. The soles of the shoes must have been smooth."

"He knows something about forensic science." Luke let out a long breath. "I don't suppose you've got details about the shoes that were stolen from the autobarge, have you? Like, did any have smooth soles?"

"Searching."

As soon as Luke had been assigned to the high-profile case and before coming to the scene of the murders, he'd studied the existing case notes. The only surviving eyewitness was the older of the two men on the Pairing Committee. He was in the hospital, sedated, and mostly

speaking gibberish. But occasionally he mumbled something about seeing only the killer's eyes, nose, and mouth.

Malc said, "The serial numbers indicate that the boat was delivering a range of adult styles. Several had soles without a tread."

"Mmm." Luke stood in the killer's place and, in his mind, replayed Malc's recording of the massacre. Thinking about the scrap of speech that Jade had rescued, Luke asked, "Rachel said 'respect' twice when I spoke to her, didn't she?"

"She said 'respect' once and 'respected' once," Malc answered.

Luke nodded. "Interesting. I wonder if all Visionaries say 'respect' a lot."

"Not known."

"I don't suppose you can use your electronic voice recognition system to compare the part recorded in here with Rachel saying 'respect' in her apartment, can you? What are the chances that they're the same person?"

"Valid comparison is impossible. The speech recorded in here is too poor in quality and too brief."

"Thought so. If Jade had trouble with it . . ." Luke shrugged and walked to the doorway where he'd seen a shadowy reflection of the assassin. "I know what's in the case notes, Malc, but using someone else's data is like running in someone else's sneakers. Not to be trusted. I want you to do the math. Compare my height with the door and then Lost Bullet's. Give me your best estimate of his height."

"A crude comparison suggests that he or she is the same height as you. However, Lost Bullet may have worn headgear, and the thickness of the soles is unknown."

Luke nodded. "So he's my height or a little shorter, certainly not taller."

"Logged. However, I should point out that few people are taller."

"Hmm. Does your information on Ethan Loach include his height?"

"His adult dimensions are not recorded," Malc replied.

"I asked The Authorities to hide an agent in Cranleigh Walkway, near Rachel Toback's house. Has that happened yet?"

"Confirmed."

"And?"

"What do you wish to know?"

"Do I have to spell it out?"

"No. Just saying the words will suffice."

Luke grimaced. "Sometimes I could strangle you."

"That would not be possible."

"All right. I give up. Has there been a sighting of

Samuel? He'll be a couple of years older than me, I guess. If he visited Rachel, how tall is he, and did the agent follow him home?"

Malc was silent for ten seconds and then reported, "There has been no communication."

"Okay. I'm done here. Let's go."

Back at Thomas's Hospital, Luke asked Alex Foxton and Dr. Coppard if they knew anything about Visionaries, but neither of them had even heard of The World Church of Eternal Vision. Alex had received some anonymous telescreen messages that ranted about meddling with God's creations. They also contained death threats, but Alex had simply deleted them and got on with his life.

Luke spent the rest of the day visiting the offices and homes that had been damaged recently. Because the crimes weren't fresh and undisturbed, Malc found no evidence that could be entered into case notes. Luke interviewed the people who worked or lived in the targeted buildings but came up with only one significant new fact. Two offices had been attacked at exactly the same time. That meant Lost Bullet was not alone in conducting a campaign against doctors.

The razor felt light but sharp and empowering in Lost Bullet's hand. Sitting naked in his bathroom, he crossed his legs and began to work on the left one. As the blade scraped upward slowly from the ankle, it sliced every hair, leaving his leg gloriously, silkily smooth again. Lost Bullet didn't care how long it took to prepare himself. There was something so satisfying about becoming clean and ready. The slower and more methodical he was, the more he liked it. When he was satisfied, he uncrossed his legs and put his left foot back onto the tiles, momentarily wincing with pain. He held out his left arm and began to shave it from the backs of his fingers up to his armpit and shoulder.

The preparation for carrying out God's will required him to revert to a childlike state. He was erasing every hair from his body—converting himself from a man into a baby—and stripping away adult sin to regain an infant's innocence. He ran the fingers of his right hand along his left arm. The shaved skin hurt slightly, and it had lost all of its roughness. He switched the razor to his other hand and began to cleanse his right arm. While he concentrated on the surface of his skin, making it perfect, he also worked on his state of mind. By the end of the lengthy process, he would be pure of skin and pure of thought. It was the ideal condition for murder.

He peered into his huge bathroom mirror, inserted the tweezers into his right nostril, and, one by one, plucked out every single nose hair that had started to grow once more. Then he cleared his left nostril as well. He didn't even wince. He needed the pain to purify

himself. Next he pulled out the few tiny hairs that were just beginning to burst through the soft skin of his eyebrows. Then he lathered his chin, cheeks, and head and raised the razor again.

When he had eliminated all of his body hair, he was still not finished. He clipped his fingernails and toenails right back to the skin so that filth could not get underneath them. After that he treated himself to a long, scalding shower.

He emerged as a new man. A newborn, really.

All that remained was to dress himself in brand-new clothes. New underwear, socks, shirt, pants, coat, shoes. Like his thoughts, everything was clean and unspoiled by life.

Lost Bullet was ready.

Dr. Pollitt scrubbed his hands thoroughly with antibacterial soap, dried them, and then stretched the medical gloves over his fingers. "You know," he said to his nurse, "it occurs to me that surgeons should take up a life of crime."

"How come?"

"Sterile and dressed like this—to stop us from contaminating patients—we'd be great at not leaving a single clue." He pulled his mask over his face and, from behind it, added, "We wouldn't contaminate a crime scene with a single hair, fiber, saliva, blood, anything.

We'd be a forensic investigator's nightmare."

"But you might be noticed, walking around like that."

Inside his mask, Dr. Pollitt snickered. "Good point. Anyway, the patient's waiting. Let's get on with it."

Dr. Pollitt turned to head for the operating room but stopped in his tracks.

Behind him, a window of the Hammersmith Fertility Clinic shattered. The barrel of a rifle poked through the broken glass like a hypodermic needle pushing through skin.

The first bullet flew into the nurse's cheek, hit the thick bone at the base of her skull, and virtually exploded. The flattened bullet carved a track across her brain, twice the size of the piece of metal. The energy from the impact made the walls of the channel vibrate, destroying the delicate tissue. The mangled bullet emerged on the other side in a cloud of blood and splintered bone.

Dr. Pollitt could not see anything beyond the window. Maybe he was in shock, maybe the darkness outside hid the killer. More likely, he was transfixed by the rifle's barrel as it swung toward him and pointed directly at his forehead. The last sounds that he heard were a muffled cry of "Respect!" and a loud bang.

Chapter Fifteen

There was little to be learned from Lost Bullet's latest killing spree. This time Malc did find two empty cartridge cases near the broken window of the clinic, but they didn't add anything to the investigation. They were a very common make—too common to trace. Matching the ones found in the Pairing Committee room, they confirmed only that Lost Bullet had not switched to a different weapon. If there had been a flower bed beneath the window, the assassin might have left a shoe print in the soil. But outside it was all concrete, decorated with two poignant bouquets of lilies. There was no other evidence of Lost Bullet's devastating visit.

Hands on his hips, Luke stood in the entrance to the fertility clinic and said, "He's targeting the same kind of prey with the same rifle." He shook his head in frustration. Deciding what to do, Luke added, "Right. I don't have time to wait for Ethan Loach to get in touch with me. I'm going after him."

"There is no need," Malc announced. "I have just received a message from him. He has agreed to come and see you briefly at eight o'clock tomorrow morning."

Luke nodded. "Good. Tell him to come to the Central Hotel."

Luke felt a shiver of pleasure when Jade's round face appeared yet again on his telescreen. A few unruly patches of blue had appeared in her bronzed hair. For once, though, her dark eyes were not shining.

"Hi! How's it going?" he said.

"Not great."

"Why's that?" asked Luke.

"It happened today. The Pairing Committee's found me a new mate. An artist, obviously."

Hurt, Luke looked away from the large screen. When he forced himself to look back, he said, "What's his name?"

Jade shrugged. "It doesn't matter. He's not Luke Harding."

Still upset, Luke had barely shaken off his drowsiness, eaten his pomegranate, and showered before the leader of the London Visionaries arrived. He was exactly on time. Luke ushered him into his living quarters, out of sight of his working area, forensic equipment, and bagged evidence.

Ethan Loach was an imposing figure. He was almost as tall as Luke but much more plump. What really made him striking—even fearsome—was his oversize bald head. According to the information that Malc had downloaded, Ethan was 35 years old, but his shaved head made him look at least five years older. Under his

raincoat, he was dressed up in a dark suit, white shirt, and red tie.

"Rachel told me some interesting things about you," Ethan said, as if he expected to take control of the meeting.

"And I found out some interesting things about Visionaries." Luke took the two leaflets from his bureau and held them up. "It started when I got these. Rachel filled in a few more things for me. I've got to say, the Church is pulling me in like a magnet."

"You're thinking of turning away from Rationalists and becoming a Visionary?"

Immediately, Luke guessed that people who weren't part of The World Church of Eternal Vision were called Rationalists. "I'm . . . fed up. You see, the London Pairing Committee is about to pair me with a girl I don't love. She's nice. She deserves better than to be stuck with someone like me, and I want to spend the rest of my life with a girl named Jade. On top of that," Luke added, with genuine bitterness in his voice, "Jade's been promised to an artist—just because he's an artist and I'm not. It's . . . ridiculous. It's . . ." Lost for words, Luke shook his head.

"I understand your anger," Ethan replied. "Arranged marriages are a sin against God. But first things first. It's unusual, to say the least, for a forensic investigator to come to God."

"I suppose so," Luke said. Deciding to catch his visitor off guard by revealing what he'd learned from Ethan's records, Luke added, "But, given your feelings about doctors, it's not as strange as a doctor becoming a Visionary preacher."

In interviews Luke was used to people who avoided eye contact. With Ethan, it was the opposite. The preacher gazed into his eyes all of the time. Luke felt like he was the one under interrogation.

"You've looked into my past."

Luke smiled wryly. "I'm an investigator. I'm supposed to be good at it."

"You're right. Many years ago I trained to be a doctor, but I learned only the limitations and saw only the butchery. I, too, became disillusioned. Your information probably tells you that I escaped from the evil clutches of medicine shortly after residency."

Luke's father was a doctor, but Luke did not react to the idea that doctors are evil because he was more eager than ever to infiltrate the Church. "I'm with you all the way," he said, his eyes drawn to his visitor's wide, shiny forehead. "I was going to check something else out with Rachel, but I didn't get around to it. What do you think about weapons?"

"Weapons?"

"Guns and knives, for example. What's your attitude to them? What guidance can you offer?"

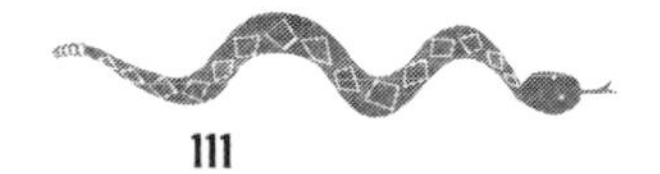

Ethan continued to stare directly into Luke's face. "We do not believe in violence against people."

Luke nodded in agreement. "That's good. I've seen too much in my line of business. But what about violence against property?"

"There is no such thing, my friend. Bricks and wood don't have feelings. They can't be hurt. A protest against a stone or wooden box is a nonviolent protest. To help God crush the curse of doctors, whites, and Pairing Committees, sometimes bricks will fall, and wood will catch on fire. So be it. That is God's will."

"That's where I draw the line as well. I don't believe in hurting people, but buildings . . . " He shrugged.

"I have to go," Ethan announced, rising to his feet. "But I am a trusting man, Luke. We're meeting tonight at the old Charing Cross Cab Station. Not the most picturesque surroundings, but the spirit will be there. You're welcome to come at eight o'clock to learn more about us. But there are two conditions. You will have to leave that behind." He jerked a thumb toward Malc.

"Fine. What else?"

"The group will need reassurance that you mean what you say. We have a way of testing your faith."

To investigate the Visionaries, Luke was desperate to penetrate the inside of the Church. "Anything," he said with a shrug and a smile. He did not realize then how much he would regret that hasty response.

As soon as the daunting visitor had left, Luke looked at Malc and said, "I didn't smell garlic. Did you?"

"I did not detect it. No."

"Any gunshot residue on him?"

"No."

"He didn't worry about his people attacking property. That makes sense," Luke said. "Quite a few Visionaries might be out and about damaging homes, offices, and hospitals—and sending death threats to Alex Foxton. That's why two places can get hit at the same time. But there's probably only one rogue Visionary attacking people."

"Speculation."

"That's why I need to infiltrate the Church."

"It is illegal and much too dangerous. In addition, if I am excluded, I cannot provide data for the investigation, and you cannot advance the case."

"True. But I'm going to do it anyway . . ."

Malc interrupted. "I strongly advise against this course of action. You are displaying irritation with The Authorities over pairing rather than following legal procedure."

It was true that Luke was not just disappointed but enraged. Two of The Authorities' Pairing Committees were forcing him and Jade to accept separate marriages. Their own heads and hearts were telling them something else entirely. Ethan Loach and his followers

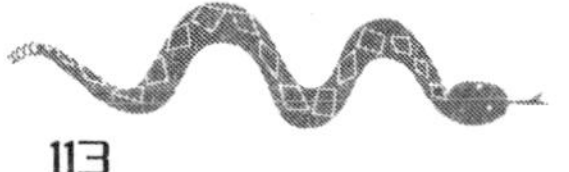

would help them resist pairing. Yet Luke had mixed feelings about The World Church of Eternal Vision because he thought that its other teachings were nonsense. To Malc, he said, "I'm doing it to meet Visionaries and get some names to investigate. That's all. I'm doing it to meet Lost Bullet. And you're staying here. End of discussion."

Chapter Sixteen

The Authorities' agent had completed her job. Because Samuel had visited Rachel that afternoon, she was able to provide Malc with photographs and a description of the twins' father. Then, by following him home, she had also discovered the address of his hostel.

Luke was tempted to follow up the agent's lead right away, but he had to curb his instinct to continue with the case. If he had gone to interview Samuel before the gathering of Visionaries that night, he would have been acting more like an investigator than a possible recruit to The World Church of Eternal Vision.

At almost eight o'clock Luke entered Charing Cross Cab Station. Without Malc, he felt naked and vulnerable. The old station had been abandoned. Occasionally, electric cabs still pulled into the waiting area at ground level, but they rarely stopped because there were so few customers to pick up now. To cross the river, the automated vehicles ran down the ramp from the surface and rushed through the tunnel. None of them was programmed to enter the underground maintenance depot because it had long since been disused.

From the station on Strand Corridor, an escalator led down to the deserted garage facilities. The steel steps

had not moved for years. The mechanism was probably clogged or corroded. Feeling ill at ease, Luke walked down, his way dimly lit by a row of safety lamps built into the side of the escalator. It felt like the descent into a cave. At the bottom there was a filthy, damp passageway. In front of him he spotted the distorted outline of two or three people before they turned right and out of his view. He decided to follow them.

Almost silently, several small black shapes flew above his head, making him duck. Recognizing them, he turned and watched the bats fly expertly over the escalator and toward the open air where, he guessed, they'd begin their nightly hunt for food.

The lights were above him now, set in the arched ceiling. Like candles, they were not powerful enough to light up the whole place, but they did guide him to the next level. Luke could tell that the tiles under his feet were littered with pieces of slushy garbage, but he couldn't see much. If Malc had been with him, the mobile would have completed an infrared scan by now and alerted him to everything in the vicinity. Luke felt as abandoned as the cab station. Somewhere water dripped monotonously. And there was the unpleasant smell of decay mixed with urine.

Nervously, he turned right into a narrower passage. He could have spread out his arms and touched the grimy walls on both sides. With a lower ceiling, the same lighting was more effective. He was burrowing deeper into the earth, but at least he could see a little better. He couldn't help but wonder what would happen if the electricity supply failed, though. It would be pitch-black, and without a flashlight or Malc, he doubted his ability to find his way back. Ahead the tunnel ended in a large underground hall. He could hear the faint sound of human voices drifting toward him. Even if the whispers had been hostile, he would have been reassured to know that he wasn't alone in the dark warren. Abruptly, the walls disappeared, and he found himself in a derelict cavern that served as a church.

Flaming torches were attached to the walls, adding to the electric lighting. The Visionaries had arranged the remaining old workbenches and contraptions in a ring where they served the purpose of seats. Some of the machines had spotlights that were once used for the more intricate jobs. In the uneven and flickering light Luke glanced around the ring.

There were 40 to 50 people. The lighting gave each one of them a shadowy, sinister face. Even so, he recognized Rachel Toback and the two boys who had given him a leaflet at Haymarket. Having seen the photographs of Samuel, Luke knew that he was the Visionary sitting next to Rachel. Then there was Ethan Loach. He was standing in the middle. All of the male members of the Church looked uncannily similar. They

were dressed in dark suits and identical red ties. And all of them had shaved heads. With his shoulder-length hair, coat, and faded blue jeans, Luke was out of place.

"Ah!" Ethan's voice boomed around the walls of the cavern, breaking the silence that had greeted Luke. "Here he is, my friends. Luke Harding."

A murmur, rather than distinct words of welcome, came from the ring of Church members. Luke got the impression that they were deeply wary of him.

"Luke deserves our understanding and sympathy. I have looked into his eyes and seen love—genuine love of a girl named Jade. The Pairing Committee hasn't taken the trouble to do the same and see what's obvious."

Now the murmurings were louder and distinctly harsh.

"Even if they had . . ." He shrugged. "They'd still condemn Luke to a life he doesn't want—a life with a different woman. And so he's turned to us." Ethan opened his arms wide and said, "Come into our circle."

Luke hoped that no one noticed that his legs were unsteady as he walked forward and squeezed between two workbenches. The men on both sides shifted a little to let him through. The features of the one on his right looked vaguely familiar, probably because he resembled every other Visionary. His baldness made his ears conspicuous. The light shining on his left side cast a long shadow of his ear on his shiny scalp, making it seem even larger.

Luke sat down where Ethan indicated and listened intently to the rest of his sermon.

"Pairing Committees would condemn Luke—and the rest of us—to living in sin because, in God's eyes, an arranged marriage is a loveless thing. It is living a lie. That's not God's way."

"Amen."

Ethan continued, "The laws of nature—the angels—know nothing about Pairing Committees. They know only about love and companionship and respect for God."

"Respect."

Luke scanned the faces of the Visionaries, wishing Malc was beside him to do the job instead. After all, Malc was the one with the photographic memory. Malc also could have scanned for gunshot residue. By now, he might have had the case solved.

"It is a simple world. First there is God. Next there are God's messengers—the angels—and then there is us. We are the receivers of God's word, the doers of his will. One day the angels will run the material world on his behalf in every way. Nothing will happen without the intervention of angels, and human beings will not try to take their place. There will be no more Pairing Committees." Ethan glanced at the newcomer and

smiled. "Come that perfect day, there will be no more weakness and no more sin. We will acquire the innocence of children. Right now we are weak and sinful, so God sends us diseases as a sign of his displeasure. Yet when that perfect day comes, there will be no more sickness and no need for doctors."

"Amen."

"Whites, too, will be a thing of the past. So great is their original sin that they wear the sign of it—the ultimate sickness—on their disfigured faces. When the world knows no sin, there will be no more genetic defects."

To Luke, it was garbage, but he did not allow his true feelings to show. He sat as if spellbound by Ethan's preaching. At least he understood the Church's hatred of white people now. Their appearance reminded Visionaries of sin. It reminded them of other people's sin and of their own.

At the end of the sermon the Visionaries mixed with each other, standing around in small groups and talking. Luke wondered if this was when some of them plotted their attacks against bricks and mortar. He suspected that only one plotted against flesh and blood, and he expected that person to keep very quiet about it.

Ethan explained to Luke that this was his chance to mingle before he made up his mind about joining the Church. Luke nodded with gratitude, but he did not mention why he was so eager to mingle.

Along with Ethan and Samuel, there were 16 other men and 19 women. None of them was taller than Luke. The rest of the Visionaries were children. For them, Charing Cross Cab Station was one big playground. Judging by their ages, some of them should have been away at school. There was no sign of the Toback twins.

Of course, Luke could not speak to all of the Visionaries, and he could not show his true colors. He wanted to ask how far each of them would go to rid London of the three curses. He wanted to ask where they were last night and what they knew about rifles. He was especially eager to find out their full names and ask about Sarah Toback's death. But he didn't ask any important questions. He could display a natural curiosity about them, but he couldn't go further and conduct an interrogation. Some of them were so wary that they didn't even give him a first name. It was like they were holding back until Luke made his membership official.

After mingling for 15 minutes he discovered that The World Church of Eternal Vision didn't attract a single type of person. They were all different. Some, like Ethan, were brash about their beliefs. They continued to rant and rave. Some were as reserved as Rachel, listening but hardly saying a word. Some just wanted to complain about the awful weather. They were a social mix, just like the people they called Rationalists.

When Ethan Loach called them to order, Luke knew that his time had come. He was encircled by members of the Church, trapped in the ring with Ethan. "This morning I told you that God—and all of us here—need to be convinced of your purpose and your faith. I told you that we've got a test."

There was a quiet gasp from a few of the Visionaries.

Trying to make light of it, Luke said with a nervous grin, "Does it involve a pair of scissors?" He grabbed a handful of his plentiful hair and said, "I couldn't help noticing . . ."

Ethan's smile was more of a smirk. "No. We believe we are closer to godliness if we are clean, like a child. But that's for later. First things first." He walked out of the circle, bent down, and picked up a wicker basket that was lurking ominously in the shadows.

Returning to the fold, Ethan said, "If you are at one with God and the angels, you will be at one with all of his creatures." He put down the basket and opened it very carefully. "Including this one."

The flattened head of a curious rattlesnake rose up from the box, and again a murmur came from the Visionaries. The creature was pale brown with dark diamond shapes running along its body. It flicked out its tongue like it was licking its lips in anticipation.

Chapter Seventeen

Luke had seen rattlesnakes in Birmingham. There they were always behind a glass panel. He had never seen anyone get close to one, and he knew that if someone did, they would always wear protective clothes. Perhaps Ethan's snake was used to seeing Visionaries close up, but it was still a wild animal—one of the most dangerous in the world. The sight of it brought out Luke's fight-or-flight impulse. He wanted either to kill it or to run away. The hardest thing was to do neither.

"I wouldn't ask you to do anything that I'm not prepared to do myself," Ethan was saying. Theatrically, he stripped off his jacket and rolled up one shirt sleeve, revealing a hairless arm. Then, moving slowly and smoothly, he got down in front of the rattlesnake as if he was going to worship it. Instead he placed his shaved, bare arm on the rim of the basket like an offering.

The snake bent down its head and brushed its lower jaw across Ethan's flesh but made no attempt to bite him. Obviously, it didn't feel threatened by him.

Ethan turned his head toward Luke. "You see? Those who arrange marriages or live in sin, doctors, whites, and the unfaithful could never live in harmony with one of God's most poisonous and aggressive creatures." He was whispering to avoid alarming the rattler. "But it won't strike the faithful. The angels protect those who

are at one with God and nature." Gingerly, Ethan rose to his feet and began to cover his arm again. To Luke, he said, "This is where you get to make your choice." From his pocket, he took out a piece of paper that looked like a page from a small notepad and dangled it from his fingers. "You can leave right now and never get to see this—the address of our next meeting place. Or you can take the challenge—do exactly what I did—and confirm your faith. There is a third possibility, of course. If you fail the test, you face God's punishment. You will remain here forever."

Every instinct told Luke to get out, but that way he'd probably blow his best chance of solving the murders. He swallowed, took a deep breath, and removed his coat. With trembling fingers, he pulled up his shirtsleeve.

The gathered Visionaries sat stiffly, watching him in complete silence.

Luke took four measured steps toward the basket, wishing he'd instructed Malc to come for him if he hadn't returned to the hotel by an agreed time. Then his mobile could have had antivenin delivered and injected within two hours. Even if he was about to be bitten, Malc could have saved his life. But Luke hadn't made any such arrangement. For once, he was on his own.

He crouched down, getting closer and closer to the snake. He was easily within its striking distance, and he felt sweat running down his back and face. The reptile looked more animated now, but its dark eyes were curiously dead. Luke ignored the flickering tongue. That wasn't the problem. It was the fangs that he had to worry about. They were as sharp as hypodermic needles, ready to inject deadly venom. In Luke's previous investigation a suspect had pulled a knife on him. The snake's fangs were much worse, much more lethal than steel. And a snake didn't care if Luke lived or died. It was just a matter of whether it could be bothered to strike.

Luke tore his eyes away from the rattler and looked at his own arm. It was not smooth like Ethan's. Would the snake be irritated by the tickly feel of hair? Could it smell his sweat and fear? Could it detect his warmth or racing heartbeat? Just for a moment Luke thought about Georgia Bowie. She knew all about snakes and biology. She could have told him what to do and what to avoid. But, like Malc, she was somewhere else. He knew only that he must not make himself a threat to the watchful reptile.

Inching his arm toward the basket, Luke knew for sure that the Visionaries had put Sarah Toback through this test after she had sacrificed her principles by taking her conjoined twins to Thomas's Hospital. He also knew for sure that she had failed. Her death had not been an accident.

As his arm settled on the cold wicker, the snake's gray tail came up out of the basket with a rustling noise. In the audience Rachel caught her breath. The rattle poked up in the air as a warning, but it remained still and silent.

Luke tried to keep his head as far away from the basket as possible. He imagined that one drop of sweat falling from his cheek and landing on the snake—or one trailing hair—would be enough to scare it into attacking.

The rattlesnake moved its head along his exposed arm as if it was smelling him or looking for something. Twice, its scaly body came into contact with his skin.

Luke gritted his teeth and refused to react to the touch. He was sure that if he pulled back suddenly, the snake would attack. It would dart forward with the speed of a missile, reveal its curved fangs, and sink them effortlessly into his arm. The poison would ooze down the grooves in its fangs and into his body. Unless he was treated quickly, death would be inevitable. Luke had seen the awful effects of rattlesnake venom on a human being. He knew that his death would be ugly and painful. Kneeling by the basket, he had to fight his natural inclination to run away. There was no doubt in his mind that he wouldn't get very far.

He waited for a few seconds, until he couldn't take any more, and then began to withdraw his arm.

Suddenly, the snake sounded its rattle as if angered that Luke was reclaiming the gift of flesh. At once, the tension in the room doubled because the noise was a chilling prelude to a bite.

The hair along Luke's arm was standing on end. He knew he was swaying slightly—he couldn't help it—but he strained to keep control so that he didn't topple over. If he did tumble, he was sure that he'd provoke an attack, and that would be the end. Steadying himself as best as he could, he tried once more to pull back little by little without disturbing the snake.

He had forgotten about the audience of Visionaries, Ethan, and even his case. He concentrated only on widening the gap between himself and the rattlesnake without making a single hasty movement. While he did this, the creature stared at him as if it was displeased but not angry enough to strike. When he thought he was far enough away, when he thought he was safe, Luke got to his feet and staggered back, far away from the basket. It was all he could do to remain upright on unstable legs. But it was over, and he had survived.

The snake settled itself back into its basket when Ethan approached it, holding out the lid like a shield. The rattler seemed to be content. It probably welcomed the return to solitude.

When the cover came between the poisonous reptile and the room, there was a collective sigh of relief.

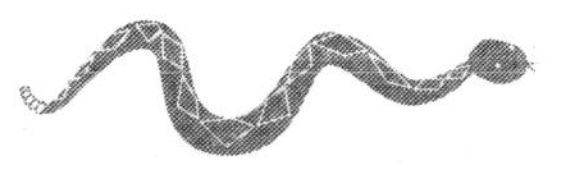

Luke's sigh wasn't the loudest, but it was the most heartfelt. He lurched to a spare place on one of the workbenches and almost fell onto it.

Ethan said, "My friends, The World Church of Eternal Vision has a new member. Welcome, Luke Harding. You are saved!"

A brief ripple of applause went around the ring, saluting the strength of his faith.

Ethan tore up the piece of paper bearing a new address. "If you'd left us or failed the test, we wouldn't have been able to return here. But, for now, this is our new church." He hesitated and then added, "It's not grand, like a Pairing Committee chamber, but it's what we do here—not the decoration—that's important. God forgives a dark and grubby home but never a dark and grubby heart."

The challenge completed and the rattlesnake caged, some members began to melt away. Most stayed behind and clustered around Luke, their mood suddenly lifted. Catching the smell of garlic, Luke realized that it was coming from Samuel. The twins' father had also put on a stylish sheepskin coat. Luke's spine tingled. He was sure he'd identified one of the bandits—and maybe Lost Bullet as well. But he didn't dare show any sign of being interested in Samuel. He couldn't afford to ruin his newly gained trust by bouncing right back into the role of forensic investigator. Instead he chatted excitedly about becoming a Visionary.

Later, on the way back through the underground tunnels, Ethan pulled Luke to one side and said, "You know, you'll be very useful to the Church. We've never saved an investigator before." He laughed. "Despite your age, that makes you the most powerful Visionary, in a way." Suddenly serious again, he added, "I wouldn't expect any of your new friends to be arrested for protests like smashing up doctors' offices or Pairing Committee rooms. Do I make myself clear?"

Luke nodded. "But what if someone was inside? What about murder? You—we—don't believe in violence against people."

In the dim passageway Ethan didn't answer right away. He stared ahead at the frozen escalator that sloped back up to the normal world. Then he said, "That's right. Murder's different. Much as we'd like to stamp out evil, killing is not for us to decide. It's a sin."

In the hotel lobby the cheerful receptionist said, "Good evening, FI Harding."

Luke nodded. "Back at work? Last I heard, you were sick."

Mr. Morgan replied, "Thank you for enquiring, sir. I've just reported for duty. It's all this wet weather. Just a cold or a germ of some kind. The doctor gave me something for it, so I'm perky enough now." As quick as

ever, he smiled and added, "No excuse to avoid the night shift, I'm afraid."

As Luke went up to his room, he realized that he should also feel cheerful. He had opened up several lines of enquiry inside The World Church of Eternal Vision, and he was still alive. He burst into his quarters and said, "I'm a Visionary!"

Malc hesitated before responding. "Only after enduring considerable nervous tension, stress, or exhaustion."

Luke halted at once, horrified. "How do you know that? You didn't have me bugged, did you? That would've put me at risk, to say the least, if I'd been found out."

"No. I detect copious amounts of fermenting perspiration, with butanedione as the major odor component."

Luke sighed with relief and smiled. "So you've scanned me for sweat."

"I analyzed the gases you are emitting."

"Nice. All I'll say is that there was a reason for copious amounts of sweat. Industrial-strength deodorant wouldn't have covered it up. And, yes, I can confirm that the Visionaries have got a rattlesnake. Now, before I take a shower and collapse, record what I say, Malc. I want to describe everyone I remember and give you a few names."

"I cannot include them in case notes."

"Fine. I just want a record," Luke said. "And first

thing in the morning I'll want you to link me to the department in charge of issuing identity cards. I've got a feeling that I'll need Owen Goode on my side before long."

Chapter Eighteen

Hands tucked behind his head, Luke pondered the enormity of space. Lying on the bed, he studied the pretend night sky projected across the ceiling. Stars always made him realize that his own planet was a mere speck of dust in a vast and mysterious universe. It also reminded him that, as an FI, he was often looking for one significant speck of dust—a mere trace—at a crime scene that had no obvious boundaries. Even when a murder had been committed inside a building, the most significant clues could be outside, somewhere between the killer's home and the victim's body. He thought of the bullet that had passed through Anna Suleman's head. Now it could be anywhere within the swollen Thames river in Westminster, the sewer system, and the open sea.

Sometimes, when Luke was feeling down, the night sky made him realize that he was a mere speck of dust in the universe as well.

He said, "It's hard to believe that one being—God—could have created all of this, as well as bacteria, humans, and all life in between."

"It is much more likely that people invented God than that God invented people," Malc replied.

"That's an opinion. You don't give opinions."

"It is listed as a fact in my encyclopedia."

Luke glanced at his mobile and smiled. "No wonder the Visionaries don't like you. They're an illegal organization, and you're the ultimate Rationalist. No hope of converting you." He paused and sighed. "Now that you've brought me back down to earth, I want you to get that agent back outside Rachel Toback's place. I'd like to visit Rachel—to say thanks for the introduction to the Church—when I know Samuel's there. I want it carefully planned to look like a coincidence."

"Transmitting request."

"Since I got back from the Church I've been thinking. Yesterday I said Lost Bullet must know something about forensic science, but I might be wrong. Maybe he hasn't left any hairs behind because he hasn't got any. Male Visionaries shave themselves at regular intervals. Completely bald. The girls and women don't shave, though. They lose hairs now and then. Your analysis in Russell Plaza proves that."

"Lost Bullet might wear a hood or a bandanna."

"Yeah, I know. Nothing's certain yet. But it's got to be a Visionary. That way, the motive and the cry of 'Respect!' make sense. You've got a record of all of the hospital staff Anna Suleman met in the last week, don't you?"

"Confirmed."

"Well, I don't think I'm going to need it. No

Visionary is going to work in a hospital. But I should go through all the stuff at 72 Russell Plaza. That might give me some extra juice. I could get pictures from the computer, but for now, why don't you just read the list to me?"

"Illogical question. There is nothing to prevent me from reading the logged items," Malc replied.

Luke winced and shut his eyes. "Go on then."

Malc rattled through the list uninterrupted until he reached the vegetation detected in the room. Most of the finds were ordinary leaves and seeds, probably blown into the house by the wind or carried in on shoes or clothing. Two of the items caught Luke's attention.

"Hang on. You said part of a leaf from the *Papaver* genus. That's a poppy, isn't it?"

"Confirmed."

"Fair enough. I've seen poppies around, but there was a piece of a seed capsule from *Papaver somniferum*. I don't think that's native here."

"Correct. It is grown under greenhouse conditions for its seeds. It is a food flavoring with a nutty taste, especially popular on bread."

"That's not all, is it?"

"The unripe seed capsule can be harvested for morphine, but it is against the law."

"Mmm. Sounds like at least one Visionary is into spices or prohibited painkillers. I guess it's okay for a

Visionary to take morphine because one of God's plants makes it, not a doctor. I don't know if it's got anything to do with Lost Bullet though."

Luke did not spot any other interesting items from the Russell Plaza address. Instead he changed direction. "There's something else I've been thinking about: the attack on Clement School. Was that arson by a group of Visionaries, or was it attempted murder by Lost Bullet?"

"Insufficient evidence."

"If it was Lost Bullet, I would've expected to see him at the door with a rifle, gunning down everyone the fire flushed out. Maybe the presence of an FI scared him off."

"Speculation."

"Mmm. Puts a question mark over the big, bald bouncer though. I didn't see him at the Charing Cross church, but I don't think every member was there. Anyway, how did the Visionaries—or Lost Bullet himself—find out where and when the whites were getting together?"

"They are not an illegal organization. They would not have to keep meetings secret."

"No, but with these arson attacks going on, I bet they're careful who they tell." He hesitated and then said, "I've got a few questions for Cleo McGrath."

"Do you want a connection now?"

In London Luke had no one to see—not for social

reasons, anyway—and nothing to do except work or sleep. "It's late, but she'll be eager to speak to me. Yes. Sound only will do."

Malc established a link within two minutes.

Cleo seemed surprised to hear from him but was pleased. "Investigator Harding. How can I help you?"

"It's that guard you had on the door at Clement School. Have you used him before?"

"Quite a few times recently," she answered.

"Do you trust him?"

"Yes. Absolutely. I went to school with him, and he lives in the apartment upstairs. He's fine."

Luke was inclined to agree with her. If the bouncer had been Lost Bullet, he would have barred the exit from the school or started shooting. "If he's upstairs, check whether he saw someone prowling around, especially if it was someone bald or hooded, and let me know. "

"I'll see him in the morning."

"Okay. Thanks."

"Is that all?" she asked.

"How do you tell your friends about meetings? Do you put up notices?"

"We used to but not now. I just use telescreen messaging."

"So how does someone like Owen get to hear about them?"

"He checks for messages now and then in a community center."

"I wonder how the people attacking you get to hear about them," said Luke.

"I can only think that they hack into our computer systems."

"Possible," Luke replied. "But not easy. It strikes me that it's more likely that they know someone white."

Cleo seemed shocked by the thought. "You mean, somebody's leaking the information?"

"Exactly."

"I can't imagine . . ."

"It may not be deliberate. I'm not saying that. But there's a way to pin it down. Would you cooperate, even if it was a bit . . . demanding?"

"We'd all cooperate. We don't want to live in fear anymore. That's more demanding than you can imagine."

"Okay. How many people do you send the message to?"

"37."

"Plus the security guard?" said Luke.

"Yes. 38."

"Right. Leave it to me."

Malc disconnected the link.

No longer contemplating the fake sky, Luke swung his legs over the edge of the bed. "I wonder how many agents The Authorities would let me have."

"Do you want me to find out?" asked Malc.

"No. I just want you to put in a request for a minimum of 190."

"That would be the largest operation in London in the last decade."

Luke shrugged. "To take down a big killer, I need a big operation. Here's the plan. The Authorities give me 38 different locations for meetings on the same night. I get Cleo to send a different address to each white and tell them not to discuss it among themselves. At the last minute she cancels all of them so no one shows up and puts themselves at risk. I send at least five agents to each address and see if and where Lost Bullet appears. When he shows up, they might catch him. Great. End of story. But if they just see him, I get a description and, what's more, I know which white person he got the information from. That'll get me really close to him. It's a good plan."

"But not completely dependable. Lost Bullet may not use the opportunity to murder whites."

"I bet he will. Especially after I stir things up at the Church meeting tomorrow. Don't forget, he's killed three medics and butchered a Pairing Committee. Whites are bound to be his next target."

"Speculation."

"Just send in the plan and my request."

"Transmitting."

Chapter Nineteen

Before breakfast on Saturday Luke stood in the middle of the living area and braced himself. Needing to prepare for the evening meeting of The World Church of Eternal Vision, he said to Malc, "I want you to fly at me and hit me."

"Where and with what velocity?"

Luke smiled. He knew that his mobile wouldn't question the order because it wasn't illegal. Even so, Malc's indifference to the strange command was unsettling. "Calculate where to hit me on the face, hard enough to give me an impressive black eye but not too much pain, if you don't mind."

"Calculation completed. Are you ready?"

"Yes. Get it over with, and then I'll recover with a pomegran . . ."

Malc crashed into him, hitting him just above the cheekbone. "Ouch!" Luke staggered back under the impact, but he didn't fall over. He exhaled and touched his throbbing face. "Thanks," he said. "Not too bad. I hope you got it right. I need a good bruise."

"The skin is injured sufficiently to cause some internal bleeding. Losing oxygen, the blood will turn dark blue. That color will be the bruise. Later the hemoglobin will decompose to brown, green, and then yellow bile pigments before the repair is completed."

"Good. That'll set me up nicely."

Luke's second bruising came when he returned to his room after breakfast, but this time it wasn't physical. Malc announced, "The Authorities have turned down your plan to trace Lost Bullet because it requires an excessive number of agents."

"No! That's just . . . pathetic. I bet Birmingham would've given me twice that number."

"Irrelevant."

Luke shook his head in frustration and swore under his breath.

Malc said, "However, they have stationed the same agent outside the Toback house, as requested."

"Very generous," Luke muttered sarcastically.

"She will inform me as soon as she sights Samuel."

Cleo McGrath did not have any useful information for Luke either. Through Malc, she told him, "Our bouncer chased away a group of teenagers, but that's all. Most of the time he was at the door, keeping out anyone suspicious rather than checking for people creeping around the back of the school."

"He didn't wander around or see smoke?"

"I'm afraid he was in the entrance hall sheltering from the weather at the time."

"I see." Luke didn't ask any more. He let his tone

express his disappointment in the security guard. Before finishing the call, though, he found out from Cleo that Owen Goode would be at Soho Community Center all morning.

At least Luke had more success with requesting an identity card for Owen. It was enough for The Authorities that a forensic investigator and his mobile aid to law and crime were both willing to vouch for a boy who had assisted a major investigation. They were even more impressed to hear that Owen Goode might be persuaded to lure the culprit into a trap. Such a cooperative citizen deserved to take a full part in London society with a valid identity card. It would be delivered to the Central Hotel before the end of the day.

"Right," Luke said. "My plan for ambushing Lost Bullet is back in business. But this time small is beautiful. Forget the agents. We'll do it on our own, Malc. Or almost on our own. We need one meeting place and one white person as bait."

It wasn't much of a community center, but at the back there was a small courtyard surrounded by brick walls. There, in the drizzle that had replaced the teeming rain, Owen was acting as referee in an improvised game of four-on-four soccer with some young boys. For a while Luke peered out from a doorway, watching but not encroaching on the action.

Owen was shouting encouragement, never criticism, at each of the boys in turn. Luke was impressed that he knew all of the players by name. Taking the place of a real sports instructor, Owen was probably doing a better job.

As soon as Luke stepped into the fray, he was almost bowled over in the rush to get away. He felt like he'd stumbled into a favorite roosting place, scaring and scattering every single bird from the area. Within seconds, he was standing in a dismal courtyard with only Owen for company. Startled by the effect he'd had on the game, he asked, "What happened?"

Owen smiled at Luke's innocence. "They don't like school, so they come here. They're all right—good kids. But they'll think an FI's come to take them back. Or most likely arrest them for the trouble they get into."

"Sorry. I only came to tell you about your identity card."

Owen looked surprised. "Oh. I didn't think you'd . . . what about it?"

"You can have it tomorrow."

His eyes narrowed with suspicion. "What's the deal?"

"Let's go inside," Luke said, opening the door again.

The center boasted a tiny kitchen, a few working computer terminals with a telescreen in between, and a game room. Three elderly women were drinking tea. A man was reading his telescreen messages, and two girls were playing ping-pong. The place was messy, but it wasn't a pigsty, and it seemed to keep the weather out.

"I need your help," Luke admitted quietly.

"So the card's a bribe."

"I wouldn't put it like that but . . ."

"Don't like the sound of it. Tell you what. We'll play pool for it instead. One game. You win, you keep the card. I win, I take the card and run."

Luke shook his head. "It's not going to work like that. What's the problem with helping out? I'll get to arrest the person who shot you."

"Sounds dangerous to me." Owen pointed to Luke's bruised eye with his still-bandaged hand.

"I bumped my head on Malc, that's all. And I haven't told you what I want you to do yet."

"Afraid to take me on, huh?"

"All right," said Luke. "But here are the rules. If you win, you get the identity card, no strings attached. If I win, you get the card after you've helped me out."

Less sure, Owen hesitated. Looking at Malc, he asked, "Is he any good at pool?"

Malc replied, "I respond only to . . ."

"It's okay, Malc," Luke said. "You can answer him."

"Searching." A few seconds later the mobile announced, "I have no data on his skill level at this game."

Luke cut in quickly before Malc could tell Owen that he had a knack for sports requiring careful aim. "Is it a deal?" he asked.

Owen thought about it for a few moments and then, showing his confidence again, said, "I'll set it up." While he positioned the triangle of balls, he said, "No cheating this time. And that," he said, nodding toward Malc, "isn't allowed to give you any tips."

"Never crossed my mind," Luke lied.

Twenty minutes later, having lost the game, Owen agreed to meet Luke in the same community center early the following morning.

Luke looked into Owen's face and trusted him.

Chapter Twenty

Luke took off as soon as the agent in Cranleigh Walkway reported that she had spotted Samuel. While Luke ran, rain beat down on his coat and hood. At Euston Plaza he slowed to a walk so that he would not appear breathless when he arrived at Rachel's apartment. With his identity card, he opened the front door of the house and then sprang up the stairs to the top floor. He did not march straight into Rachel's set of rooms but instead banged on her door.

Rachel was astounded. She stared at him, from top to bottom, and then stood to one side. "You'd better come in. You look like a drowned rat."

"Thanks. I just came to say thank you for . . . oh. Sorry, it's . . . Samuel, isn't it?"

Samuel was cradling the twin brothers, one resting on each arm. He glanced at Malc and then at Luke. He nodded his head in a guarded greeting.

"Sorry," Luke said, jerking a thumb toward Malc. "We're both dripping."

Neither Rachel nor Samuel said a word.

"It's all right," he said, emerging from his coat. "It's purely social, not business. Mind you," he added, looking at Samuel, "I'm glad you're here. I was going to warn you."

“Warn me? What about?”

“Don’t panic. I think I can smooth it over.” Luke dropped into a chair.

“Smooth what over?”

“An autobarge got ransacked the other day. Monday, it was. The investigator in charge has come up with a few names, and I’m afraid yours is one of them.” Luke hoped that neither of them would realize that he didn’t know Samuel’s last name.

“Mine?”

Luke nodded. “I’m having a word with her. I think I can . . . you know . . . put her off. But first, you’d better tell me if you were one of the bandits.”

Samuel exchanged a guilty expression with Rachel but did not respond.

“It’s okay. I know how you feel. No one got hurt. A few people up north had to live without new coats, shoes, and fruit. So what? They’ll survive.”

Samuel glanced down toward his children. “I’ve got kids to care for. I’ve got to do what’s best for them.”

Luke noted that the backs of Samuel’s hands were as hairless as the twins’. “Sure. Don’t worry about it. If all else fails, I’m pretty good at hacking into computers and altering lists of names before they go off to The Authorities. It’s only fair that I help a fellow Visionary. By the way, were any other Visionaries in on it? Am I going to have to help out someone else if another name crops up?”

"No. I was the only one from church."

"Fine. There's just one thing . . ."

"What's that?" asked Samuel.

"Well, I am investigating a murder. I talked to Ethan about it, and he thinks I'm doing the right thing. Murder's a sin."

"What's it got to do with me?"

"Nothing," Luke replied. "It's just that it happened outside Thomas's Hospital near that barge—and more or less at the same time. You didn't happen to see anything suspicious, did you?"

Samuel shook his head.

"Did you see a woman coming out of the hospital?"

"No."

"Were any of the bandits carrying weapons?"

"I don't," Samuel replied, "but the others do. All of them."

"What type of weapons?" Luke asked.

One of the babies stirred, opened its eyes, and coughed before settling down again. "Knives mostly. A couple have stingers, I think."

Luke grimaced. "That's not God's way, is it? Any other type of guns?"

Samuel shrugged. "I don't think so."

"Did you hear a shot being fired?"

Samuel smiled. "No chance. There was a thunderstorm going on. You don't hear anything else when God roars."

"Respect," Luke murmured.

Getting bolder, Samuel said, "You look like you've been in some trouble."

Luke touched the bruised skin around his eye. "No problem. I got into an argument with a white boy, and he started on me. No huge harm done, but he got away. Still, I know where he lives. I won't forget. Anyway . . ." He stood up and began to put his coat back on. Smiling at Rachel, he said, "I only came to say thanks for introducing me to Ethan and the Church, and here I am, talking about a case when I promised I wasn't going to. I'll see you both tonight. Okay?"

"Yes," they answered simultaneously.

Outside again, passing a sodden Euston Plaza, Luke said, "The Authorities can have their ransacked autobarge back again. I'm finished with it. Release it, Malc."

"Transmitting message."

"And I don't think I'll need the evidence you recorded on board. I'm sure it's got nothing to do with Lost Bullet now." He paused and then said, "I didn't smell any garlic around Samuel this time, but I bet you did."

"Confirmed."

"How about gunshot residue?"

"I did not detect any traces."

"I can't stop you from reporting Samuel as a bandit, can I, Malc?"

"No. My programming requires me to transmit his confession to The Authorities."

"All right. But add a note. It's very important. Right now they can't do anything like arrest him or question him because, if they do, they'll ruin my murder investigation. They'll probably get me killed as well. Got that?"

"Logged."

Luke spent lunchtime talking to Dr. Coppard, updating him on the progress of the investigation into his wife's death. Then Luke persuaded him to give up his apartment in Marylebone Freeway tomorrow.

The doctor shrugged as if the quarters he'd shared with Anna Suleman meant nothing to him now. "If you think you can catch her killer there, it's yours. I spend most of my time at the hospital anyway. I'm working it out of my system, you see. It's the only way to stop the grief from overwhelming me."

Luke nodded sympathetically. "I'll let you know how it goes."

In the afternoon Luke moved on to the psychiatric ward. There he learned nothing from the barely conscious fourth member of the Pairing Committee. But one of the nurses was especially helpful. "He put his hand up and touched my cheek this morning," she told Luke, mimicking her patient's action with her own hand. "Then he said, 'Smooth, like a woman's.' I smiled and said, 'I am a woman,' but he just looked puzzled. 'No. Him. The one who . . .' He said something like, 'Just his eyes, nose, and mouth. That's all I saw. Smooth, like a woman.' That was the gist of it anyway."

"You definitely think he was talking about a man?"

"Certain."

"He wasn't confused, talking about a woman?"

The nurse shook her head. "He said 'him' or 'his' at least twice. Besides, he wouldn't say, 'Like a woman,' if it was a woman, would he?"

Luke nodded and smiled. "Thanks. That's useful."

When Luke returned to the hotel in the early evening, Mr. Morgan broke off a conversation with Elodie to call him over to the desk. "You've had a delivery," the receptionist said, taking an envelope from a mailbox and thrusting it toward him.

"Thanks," Luke replied, feeling the rigid plastic of an identity card through the paper. "You're looking healthy and well."

"Thank you, sir. I'm fine. Anything else I can do for you before I go off duty?"

"Not at the moment," said Luke as he headed

for the elevator.

Almost as soon as he walked into his apartment and sat down, the telescreen came to life. Jade peered out of the wall at him and cried, "What have you been doing?"

"What do you mean?"

"You've got a black eye!"

"Oh, that. You should see the other guy. Actually, it was Malc, and I put a really big dent in his armor plating."

"That is incorrect . . ."

"Now you've spoiled it," Luke said to Malc. "There goes my hard-man image." He turned back to the telescreen. "We bumped into each other. That's all."

Jade looked at him severely. "You're planning something, FI Harding."

"Sound technicians make noise; investigators make plans."

"Huh? Sound technicians analyze noise too. Assistant Forensic Investigator Jade Vernon's been at it again."

"Oh?" Luke prompted, suddenly alert.

"I've been trying out some more enhancements on that awful recording you sent me. You know, after the last gunshot there's something faint. Very, very faint. I can only just pick it up before chaos kicks in, but there are footsteps."

"That's Lost Bullet retreating. I guess he took off after doing 75 percent of the job because he heard people coming. So?"

"Well, I've been recording a lot of people starting to run and doing comparisons with your soundtrack," said Jade.

"And?"

"Your man doesn't run evenly. His timing's out, and he moves more heavily on one side than the other."

"Are you saying that he's got a limp?"

"Yes. Real or faked, I don't know, but there's a definite limp there."

Luke hesitated. He was thinking that a limp might mean Lost Bullet had a pain in one leg, and that might mean he used morphine from poppy seed capsules.

"Luke?"

"Yes?" he replied.

"Take care. Don't do anything sudden. Every time I listen to that soundtrack, I get a really bad feeling."

Chapter Twenty-One

This time Luke knew where he was going, so the underground tunnel seemed less threatening. Yet he was still nervous. He feared what would happen if the Visionaries discovered that he was a fraud. Without Malc, he felt like he'd left a piece of himself behind. The mobile had been designed to enhance Luke's ability to see, hear, and smell. Without those heightened senses, Luke was as weak—and as strong—as any 16 year old. Even if he identified Lost Bullet at the Church, without Malc to oversee the procedure and uphold the law, he could not act.

Behaving like a new and eager recruit to the Church, he showed up early. His real goal was to watch the members arriving, hoping to spot a man with a limp. Maybe it was because of the poor lighting in the cavern, maybe it was because the Visionaries entered in groups, but Luke didn't notice anyone walking unevenly.

Ethan Loach's sermon wasn't a repeat of the previous day's. He concentrated much more on God's love of his creations, rather than his punishments. Much to Luke's relief, the Church's snake did not make a guest appearance this time. And during his animated preaching Ethan Loach did not show the slightest hint of a limp as he paced back and forth.

Even if he had been among friends, Luke would have felt awkward. His mass of hair and lack of Church uniform—dark suit, light shirt, and red tie—made him the odd one out. He hoped that his lack of faith was not also visible to everyone.

Afterward Luke and his black eye became the center of attention for a while.

"Even in this light, I can see that's a beauty," Ethan said. "What happened?"

Luke pretended to be coy. "I'm not sure I should . . ."

"I think you should," Ethan replied with a smile.

"I . . . uh . . . I got knocked around by a white boy."

There was a quiet gasp among his audience.

It was going to plan. Luke had got most of the Visionaries around him. He shook his head. "Maybe I was asking for it, I don't know, but I saw him bullying two little boys in Regent's Common, calling them all kinds of names. I stepped in and asked him a few questions. Found out he's training to be a doctor. He gave me the creeps . . ." Luke pointed to his bruise.

"You're an FI. What are you going to do about it?"

"I didn't have my mobile with me, so I've got no proof," Luke replied. "There's nothing I can do. As far as the law's concerned, he's in the clear." Hoping that Lost Bullet was listening, he added, "But I know where he lives—in that huge concrete tower on Marylebone Freeway—and he messes around in Regent's Common.

Next time I pay him a visit I'll have my mobile."

The gathering fractured into smaller bunches, and then gradually each cluster broke up as Visionaries drifted away. First Rachel and Samuel left, probably to see to the twins. Samuel walked perfectly. Mostly the members strolled out in groups of two, three, or four. One man, though, left alone. And he limped.

Luke could see only his back. He was about to follow when Kurt—probably the oldest Visionary in the Church—gripped his arm. In his other hand Kurt held a walking stick.

The old man said, "It's so good to see some new blood coming in. The youth of today, they're just not the same. They're behind all this lawlessness. They don't have respect for God and his law. Not like you."

"True," Luke answered. He was desperate to leave, but it was too dangerous for him to act suspiciously—like an investigator. He couldn't just dash away. Besides, Kurt still held his left arm. Glancing over Kurt's shoulder, he asked, "Do you know who that is?" He pointed, just before the man limped out of view. "I spoke to him earlier, but it was embarrassing because I didn't know his name."

"Ah, my eyes. They're not what they used to be either. But . . . uh . . . I think it was Reece."

"Reece?"

"Yes."

"Reece what?"

"He keeps himself to himself. You know, now that I think of it, I've never heard his last name. I just know him as Reece. He's a good man, though."

"Thanks. It'd be good to chat to him some more if I can catch up to him."

Kurt smiled. "That's right, youngster. I wish I had your energy. Yes, off you go. Might as well use your legs while they're still healthy. Not even God and a good life can stop them from wearing out sooner or later." He let go of Luke's sleeve, slapped his right leg, and let out a laugh that was halfway between a wheeze and a cackle. "You won't see me getting a move on these days." In parting he said, "Respect!"

Luke was about to make a getaway when Ethan intercepted him. The preacher warned him not to champion the Church's aims so energetically that he got himself into trouble. "That wouldn't do us—or you—any good at all." Then he said, "I heard you're helping Samuel, though. That's a better way to start, Luke. Thank you."

Luke shrugged. "No problem."

"Till the next meeting then," Ethan said, his eyes fixed on Luke.

"Respect."

Luke walked away, but as soon as he was out of view of the remaining Visionaries, he sprinted as fast as the dark tunnels allowed, hoping to close in on the limping man. Yet, when Luke emerged from the cab station into the lamplight, he saw only the man's outline going west on Strand Corridor. Once more Luke took off at full speed.

He didn't get very far. Almost at once, a gang of around ten people came between him and his prey. By habit, Luke glanced over his shoulder, but Malc wasn't there. His mobile's new defensive and offensive capability would not save him. Luke was on his own. It was no use showing the mob his identity card to prove that he was an investigator. Knowing that an FI's card was very valuable, they would simply steal it. Besides, he was young, and there was no sign of a mobile aid to law and crime, so they'd probably think he had stolen the card from a real forensic investigator.

"What do you want?" said Luke.

Most of them were men, but it was one of the two women who replied. "Everything you've got."

Luke was confident that he could take on one or two of the bandits but not all of them.

They shuffled into a line and began to curve around Luke, intending to encircle him completely.

The woman said, "You got any weapons?"

For a second Luke was torn between the truth and a bluff. He decided it was less dangerous to be honest. "No."

"Shame. We could use some." The ringleader came up close to him and said, "Okay. We'll start with the coat. Take it off."

"My coat?"

"Is there something wrong with your ears? Or should I make something go wrong with them?" There was a knife in her hand.

Luke put his hands on the zipper but hesitated.

"I wouldn't try anything, if I was you," she snarled.

Luke had not unzipped his coat before some of the thugs shouted a warning to each other. Then they all began to run away down Strand Corridor in a panic.

Luke turned around to see what had scared them. Behind him, Kurt was standing in the cab tracks with a walking stick in one hand and a gun in the other.

Chapter Twenty-Two

Luke's heart pounded, and his stomach churned. Maybe he'd been chasing the wrong man. He could be facing Lost Bullet right now. Kurt might look frail, but even an old and weak Visionary could pull a trigger.

Kurt gave one of his rasping laughs and said, "You looked like you could use some help, youngster. I may be getting older, but I've got my uses, you know."

Still shaken, Luke said, "Thanks."

"I told you," Kurt muttered, "there's a lack of respect for God's law today. It needs to be fixed." He slipped the gun back into a pocket. "You can't rely on me to do it much longer. Not at my age. Well, I'm off." He hobbled toward Duncannon Walkway.

"Thanks again," Luke shouted after him.

Kurt raised his free hand but did not turn around.

In the safety of his hotel room Luke updated Malc's unofficial and patchy descriptions of Visionaries. He concentrated on Kurt and Reece, but there was little he could say about Reece. He had not got close enough to draw an accurate picture. Then Luke tried to tell Malc what he had done at the church. "I planted a few seeds. I'm betting I'll get some fruit tomorrow."

"Impossible."

"Are you grumpy because I left you on your own again?"

"I do not get grumpy about anything, but The Authorities have their concerns about your methods."

"Only because you told them."

"Correct. I do not choose to transmit details. I do not have free will. I simply execute programs."

"The Authorities will forget their concerns if I arrest Lost Bullet tomorrow—while you're there."

Luke went to bed with a head too full of hope and dread to sleep. He worried that he'd be putting Owen Goode in danger. He worried that Lost Bullet would continue his campaign of tribal cleansing. And he worried that he was out of his depth. Yet Luke felt a compulsion to continue, no matter how risky it became.

When Luke did eventually slip into a restless sleep, Ethan's rattlesnake was coiled on his chest. It stared at him with its dead eyes. In the background he heard a whisper. "The laws of nature know nothing about Pairing Committees. They know only about love and companionship." Then there was Jade's voice. "It happened today. The Pairing Committee's found me a new mate. He's not Luke Harding." In the next moment he seemed to be looking down on his own bed. Where he should have been lying he saw only a sad bunch of lilies. Beside it, where he'd hoped to see Jade and his parents, there was only Malc.

Then it was Sunday morning.

The razor made a scraping noise as Lost Bullet brought it up from the back of his neck, over the top of his head, and onto his brow. He was almost ready. When God called upon him to pull the trigger three more times, he would be pure of mind, pure of body. God would be pleased with him.

It was obvious to Lost Bullet. Luke Harding was not a convert to The World Church of Eternal Vision. He attended Church meetings in a crazy attempt to solve six murders. He was setting a trap. Lost Bullet had watched the inexperienced FI and listened to him carefully. He knew precisely what was going on. He laughed out loud. He was also certain that a mere mortal like Luke Harding would not catch him. God would not allow his good work to be challenged by a mere youngster. Lost Bullet would shatter the defiled heart of the white boy. Then he would rid the world of FI Harding. It was justified because the investigator was faking faith. He was making a mockery of the Church. And that made Lost Bullet angry. For some reason, God's snake had not struck Harding, so now it was up to Lost Bullet.

He put down the razor and picked up the tweezers instead. He leaned in toward the long mirror and plucked out the few eyebrow hairs that were attempting to grow again.

Soon. Soon.

Luke and Owen were the only ones at the community center in the early morning. Owen listened to Luke with his mouth open and a look of disbelief on his face and then exclaimed, "You're going fishing for a killer shark, and I'm your bait! That's what you're saying."

Luke shrugged. "Yeah. I guess so. But I'll do everything I can . . ."

"What if it's not enough?"

"I'm not giving you a guarantee. There's no such thing. But I'll be there, and I'll order Malc to stay with you all the time. Maximum surveillance and defense mode."

Owen shook his head. "You're no bodyguard, are you? You're an investigator. You take care of people after they've been shot, not before. I don't want to become one of your subjects."

"Malc's programming covers protection."

"He's just a machine. Not good enough."

"I am a state-of-the-art . . ."

Putting up his hand to stop Malc, Luke sighed. "How do you feel about being white, Owen?"

"How do I feel? No different from anyone else. I sure look different, but I don't feel different."

"Exactly," Luke replied. "But that's not how some see you. These people called Visionaries want to get rid of you because you've got a tiny genetic difference. According to them, that's a terrible sin. For one of them, it's a reason to kill, and if he's not stopped, he'll continue killing because he thinks he's doing the right thing. He thinks he's doing the world a favor by assassinating doctors, Pairing Committees, and white people."

"Stopping him's your job, not mine."

"True. But I need some help. I'm asking you."

"No chance. Not even for an identity card."

"Sure?"

"Certain."

Luke shrugged. "Well, I can't force you." From his coat pocket, he took out the card and held it out to Owen. "Here. You can have it anyway. It's no use to me."

Owen glanced down at the card but made no attempt to take it. Instead he gazed at Luke. "You're giving it to me even though I won't play your game?"

Luke nodded. "I saw you with those kids, setting up a soccer game for them. They looked up to you. You were doing a great job. You deserve an identity card." He handed it over, turned, and walked away moodily.

Luke was about to enter the warren of Soho walkways—a strange mixture of concrete and jungle—when Owen called out, "Wait." Walking up to Luke,

Owen said, "He stays with me?" He nodded toward Malc.

Cheering up instantly, Luke answered, "Yes. For your protection."

"He's still got that fancy zapping thing?"

Luke smiled. "A laser, yes."

"All right. You've got a deal." Owen paused before adding, "Anyhow, you'll probably get to Regent's Common in one piece if I take you. I know London."

Above them, the heavens had cleared, and the rain had finally stopped. The city was a sponge that had soaked up as much water as it could take. Even without more storms, it would remain saturated for days.

When the three of them reached the building on Marylebone Freeway, Luke unlocked the door, but Malc insisted, "I will go first."

"Why?"

"Because you are not bulletproof."

"Are you?"

"Not entirely. My scanner and sensors need outlets and inlets that cannot be protected. However, I can be repaired or replaced easily, unlike human beings."

There was no one in the lobby. When the doors of the elevator sprang back, Malc was the only one in view. Luke and Owen had flattened themselves against the adjoining wall. But it was unnecessary. The elevator was an empty box. They rode up to the 11th floor, and again, when the doors opened, only Malc went out to check that the way was clear. It was. The whole building was eerily quiet. They made their way to Anna Suleman's quarters. Luke and Owen stayed outside while Malc scanned the apartment with visible, ultraviolet, and infrared radiation. When he declared it free of living creatures, he invited the two boys to enter.

Owen looked around in awe. He was especially impressed by the bathroom. "It's got a bathtub and a shower! Fantastic. And a clean toilet and a sink." He went back into the living room and said, "So this is how it is for rich people."

Luke smiled. "Today it's how you live."

When Owen moved toward the window to get a good view over London, Luke said, "No. Stay away from all of the windows."

Owen nodded. "Good point."

Lost Bullet could have been hiding out in the derelict building on the other side of Marylebone Freeway. Right now the barrel of a rifle could be poking out of one of its broken windows, hidden by the masses of leaves.

"What do we do now?" Owen asked, sitting down. "Wait for a big, bad man with a big, bad gun to come along and kill me?"

"I don't think so," Luke answered. "Put yourself in his shoes . . ."

"No, thanks."

"He probably doesn't know which apartment . . ."

"Unless he followed us here and ran up the stairs until he got to the floor where the elevator stopped."

"The building's locked. You saw that."

"So he can shoot people, but he can't smash a window?"

"Okay. He could've got in," Luke admitted. "He might be on the other side of the door right now. But it's locked, and Malc will hear him before he can get in and fire. Anyway, I think he'll wait out there." Luke pointed out of the window. "If he doesn't know where we are inside, he'll hang around outside."

"And what's Malc going to do when he sees the bad guy?"

"If he's carrying a rifle, Malc will burn his hand until he drops it. If he tries to pick it up, he'll fry his hand again. If he's already taking aim, Malc will blind him temporarily. It's a clever laser."

"You want me to go outside, don't you? You want me to parade around making myself a target."

"No. That'd look too obvious. But I thought you might want to kick a ball around in the park."

"With you?"

Luke shook his head. "I'll be close to Malc but out of sight."

"You said he'd be with me all the time. Maximum defense, you said."

"That's right. He can protect you just as easily from a few feet away. You see, if this Visionary sees Malc or me, it's a giveaway that I've tricked him."

Trying to cheer himself up, Owen replied, "You could join me in the park if you put on a wig and a false beard."

"Sorry," Luke said with a comical shrug, "I forgot to bring my bag of disguises."

Malc interrupted. "Forensic investigators do not have a . . ."

"Anyway," Luke butted in, "if he finds out it's a trap, he'll be scared off, or he'll be angry. I don't think either of us wants to face him when he's angry."

Chapter Twenty-Three

Lost Bullet was supremely confident. He was clever; he had the element of surprise; he'd figured out Luke Harding's plan; and, of course, God was guiding him. He had forced his way into the building through the fire exit and then pushed the door back into place so that it looked undisturbed. His rifle hidden in his golf bag, he was standing next to the elevator on the sixth floor, looking out of the window toward the north. He had a perfect view over Regent's Common.

Below him, the white boy was playing alone with a soccer ball, using his feet, thighs, and head. Lost Bullet could see that he was skillful, but it was a pointless talent. Besides, he'd soon be dead. Lost Bullet couldn't see Harding, but he had little doubt that the investigator was down there somewhere. At first he hadn't spotted Malc, but occasionally the low sunlight caught something reflective in a bush near the boy with the ball.

Of the three of them, the mobile was the most dangerous. Lost Bullet wanted to put that out of action first. Then both Harding and the law would be neutralized. Lost Bullet was not going to take potshots from the sixth-floor window, though, because it was too far, and he did not have all three targets in sight. One good shot might hit the white youngster, but the blast would also be a warning to Luke Harding. The traitor would make a run for it, and Lost Bullet would not be able to complete his task. He had a much better plan. He'd figured out how he could get much closer to them but remain completely unseen.

Using the stairs, he limped up to the landing of the top floor—the 14th—where he still had a view over the park but he also had access to the loft.

Luke had walked around the outside of the building. None of the windows had been smashed. There was nothing to suggest a break-in. Malc was scanning continually with every wavelength available to his processor. He had detected five red squirrels, 23 birds, one fox, two mice, one tree snake, and 13 people. None of the humans matched the description of a male Visionary like Kurt or Reece. The boys had been out for two hours, and Owen looked bored.

"Lost Bullet hasn't shown up—yet," Luke whispered to his mobile. "Is it safe for us to go in for a while? Owen needs a break. And food, I guess."

"I do not sense a current danger. That does not mean it is . . ."

"Yeah. All right. The riskiest part is when we're all together. I'll go first and open the door. You follow with Owen after 20 seconds. Okay?"

"Confirmed."

Staying alert, Luke made his way around to the entrance. He swiped his card past the security panel, opened the door, and waited. He watched a man walking along Marylebone Freeway, but with a full head of hair, he wasn't a Visionary. And he didn't take any notice of Luke.

Malc and Owen appeared, and Luke ushered them inside right away. To go up to the 11th floor, they followed the same routine that they'd used earlier. In case they had summoned not just the elevator but a killer inside it, Luke and Owen positioned themselves out of sight of anyone coming down to ground level. Again, though, the cage was vacant. They piled in, and Luke hit the button by the number 11.

As soon as the contraption reached the first floor, Malc said, "Stop it at the next level."

"Why?" asked Luke. But he hit the button for the second floor anyway.

"The motion of the elevator is different . . ."

Malc did not have time to finish his sentence. Above them, the hatch in the ceiling opened. The man standing on top of the elevator among the whirring machinery had one foot on either side of the opening. Perched on top of them, he looked huge. It seemed a long way up to his bald head. He was poking the barrel of a rifle down into the gap.

At once, Luke threw himself in front of Owen.

Malc did not have the time to turn and focus his laser through the roof of the cage. He calculated the quickest defense and flew upward to plug the hole with his own casing.

The first bullet went straight through his sensor port and demolished his movement processor. Completely disabled, Malc crashed to the floor.

Luke looked up. Lost Bullet's chilling face grinned back at him from the gloom. It was the smile of a triumphant man, the smile of a man who didn't care which boy he killed first. He pointed the rifle at Luke's chest and squeezed the trigger.

The elevator jolted and stopped at the second floor. The gunman lost his footing and fired as he stumbled. In the tight space the discharge sounded loud enough to shatter eardrums. The bullet went straight through the base of the elevator, a few inches from Luke's left foot.

Before Lost Bullet could regain his balance and take aim again, the doors sprang open. Luke pushed Owen out, crying, "Run!"

There was another shot, but it didn't find its target. Luke didn't even look back. He knew that Lost Bullet would clamber down into the elevator, but it would be a struggle for him. By then, the cage would be on its way up again. He would have to stop it on a higher level and get out before he could follow them. Luke and Owen were young and strong. They were both good runners.

"Down the stairs! Let's get out of here!" Luke yelled. "We can lose him."

Recovering from the shock, Owen shouted back, "Follow me. This is my kind of game."

Luke noticed that Owen's face was even whiter than normal. But his expression told Luke that, after hours of waiting, he welcomed a race. It would pump the blood back into his cheeks.

Luke was used to relying on Malc. Right now he could not think of a better substitute than Owen. The boys hurtled down the stairs, trying not to go so fast that they fell. They charged out of the main door, and Owen led the way across Marylebone Freeway and down Harley Corridor. They sprinted past the row of doctors' offices. Two of them bore the marks of The World Church of Eternal Vision: they had been burned down. Owen veered right into Devonshire Walkway and immediately slammed into a gang of four girls. The young women were so surprised that they parted to let Owen through. Luke followed, skidding on the layers of slippery brown leaves. A few seconds later Owen turned left on to The Mews. The buildings on both sides closed in on them with every turn. Owen was leading them deeper and deeper into the slums of London. There they could fall prey to muggers, but the limping Visionary was surely a long way behind them.

After five breathless minutes they burst through on

to Oxford Freeway. It was like emerging into an open field from a narrow tunnel. Slowing to a walk, Owen said, "That'll do. He doesn't stand a chance."

Luke looked behind him. There was no sign of Lost Bullet and no sign of Malc either. He shook his head. Malc was only a machine, but Luke hated the idea that he was lying alone and damaged. Luke felt terrible because he had abandoned an injured friend.

"What now?" asked Owen. "Are you going home?"

"Home? No. I can't. The bad guy's bound to know that I'm at the Central Hotel. I'd be a sitting duck," Luke replied. "Really, I want to go back for Malc . . ."

Owen interrupted. "You're kidding me. The guy with the gun will be waiting for you. You set a trap. He sets a trap."

"I don't think so, but you're right, it's too dangerous. I don't have much choice. I'm going to The Authorities. They'll send out a rescue and repair team for Malc—and people to collect evidence from the elevator." He was going to add that he'd be out of harm's way with The Authorities, but his mind turned to the London Pairing Committee, and he kept quiet. Not even a committee in its own chambers was safe from Lost Bullet.

"You can give a description of your man while you're there, now that you've seen him. You know who he is."

Luke sighed heavily. "I didn't recognize him. Without Malc, I can't do anything anyway."

"You're an investigator. You arrest people."

"Yeah, I arrest them, but Malc has to agree that there are grounds for arresting and charging them, and he's got to record it to make sure that it's all done according to procedure."

"The Authorities don't trust you much. Strikes me that the machine's more important than you."

Luke nodded. "As far as the law's concerned, yes, you could be right."

"Are you going to Westminster now?"

"The sooner, the better."

"How many times do you want to be mugged on the way?" Owen said with a mischievous grin.

"None would be nice."

"I'd better come then. You want to avoid some places between here and there."

Luke returned the smile. "Thanks. Again."

At Westminster Bridge Luke needed to go one way and Owen Goode the other. Luke had to head for the Houses of The Authorities, and Owen was about to resume an uncertain life. Before they parted Luke asked, "Why did you really help me?"

Owen shrugged. "Probably because you made me feel important."

"You are," Luke replied. Then he added, "We should keep in touch."

"Oh? How?"

"You've got a clean identity card now. You can get an apartment with its own telescreen. I'll mail you through Malc . . . when he's back in action. If he ever is."

"All right," said Owen. "Good luck."

"Yeah. And you."

Everywhere Luke looked in the room there was carved mahogany. The seats had plush green cushioning. The elaborate ceiling seemed to be miles above his head. Huge oil paintings of dignitaries past and present hung on the walls. The place was so expensive and ornate that it was tacky. Luke thought about Owen. For him—and many other Londoners—the lavish room would be completely alien.

Two representatives of The Authorities were reprimanding Luke for disobeying and mistreating Malc. "Because of your reckless attempt at entrapment, the man you call Lost Bullet might be completing the destruction of your mobile right now."

Luke defended himself. "I think he'll have chased me for a while, given up, and got out of the area. He's cautious. Remember, he didn't shoot the last member of the Pairing Committee when he heard people coming. He got out instead. I don't think he'll have gone back when quite a few people will have heard shots."

"Well, we'll soon know—when the team gets to the site."

The other voice of The Authorities said, "Did your mobile capture an image of Lost Bullet?"

Luke shrugged. "I hope so."

Arms crossed in anger, the first representative snapped, "Even if it did, its memory chips may not have survived."

"Malc keeps a backup on your central computer, doesn't he?"

"Yes. But not immediately. I've just checked our computer. It's not there. If your mobile got a picture, there wasn't time to transmit it. You're relying on its memory being intact." He paused and leaned forward. "Now, about your . . . unorthodox methods."

Interrupting, Luke said, "They almost got me Lost Bullet."

"They almost got you and a member of the public shot! They certainly got a very valuable mobile incapacitated."

"Sorry."

"Sorry? Is that all you can say?"

"When I get Malc back . . ."

"*If* you get it back . . . " the bad-tempered representative said.

The second man explained, "Your mobile may be too damaged, or we may decide to dismiss you as a forensic investigator."

Speechless, Luke watched the two of them as they

huddled together and whispered to each other. He couldn't make out what they were saying, but he knew they were deciding his fate. Luke was hurt. He thought that a consideration of his future was worth more than a few snatched minutes.

"We have agreed. You will be reunited with your mobile or given another one so that you can bring this case to a satisfactory resolution. There is a condition. You will listen to the mobile's advice and act upon it from now on. No more unorthodox methods."

Luke didn't know where they'd draw the line between right and wrong. Luke himself never thought about that line; he simply did what he thought would solve a case. Even so, he agreed to the condition.

"For now, you are suspended. You will be taken to a safe room until we have a verdict on your mobile aid to law and crime."

Chapter Twenty-Four

He had been stripped of his rank and dumped in a safe room for the sin of being unconventional—and almost successful. When someone brought him a late lunch and a drink, the tiny room felt even more like a prison cell. Alone, he thought about Jade, Malc, and Lost Bullet. He hoped that the gunman hadn't turned his rage against anyone else. Luke wished he could pass the time by listening to Jade's music, but without Malc to transmit it, he couldn't puncture the silence. He thought about the case, but without Malc to monitor it, he couldn't pursue it. And he wished he could talk to Jade, but without Malc to link them together, he was isolated. Imprisoned.

Yet when the door next slid back, a mobile aid to law and crime floated in.

Luke jumped up. "Is that you, Malc?"

"Partly."

Luke could have hugged him, but he didn't because it would not have meant anything to a ball of metal. "Partly? What does that mean? I want my Malc. You're not an identical twin, are you?"

"Negative. In human terms I am the same head transplanted onto an identical body."

"So you survived! Fantastic."

"I sustained a lot of internal damage, so much has been replaced, but my main processors remained operative."

"Your memory's intact?"

"It is," Malc answered without a hint of relief or excitement.

Luke grinned. "So why did you say 'negative'? I trained you to say 'no'."

Malc answered, "Three logic boards had to be set to default values."

"Never mind. It's terrific to have you back."

"I am ready for active service, so your suspension has been lifted."

"I'm back on the case? We can go?"

"Correct."

"Great." Luke was eager to get out of his prison, but before he headed down the corridor at full speed he asked, "Come on. Tell me what I really want to know. Did you get a picture of Lost Bullet?"

"Confirmed."

"Excellent! All I've got to do now is match the picture with a Visionary. Should be easy. It wasn't Kurt. Lost Bullet's much younger. And it wasn't Samuel or Ethan." He began to stride down the wide corridor.

Malc said, "I put the image through my face recognition system and identified him."

At once, Luke halted. "You've what?"

"I have put the image . . ."

"No. You said you've identified him. How?"

"My face recognition system found an exact fit with an entry in my database. The analysis was made successful by ignoring facial hair."

Luke's heartbeat leaped. He'd gone from deep depression to elation in a matter of moments. "It really is good to have you back. Who is it?"

"Mr. Morgan, the hotel receptionist. His first name is Reece."

"What? But . . ." Luke could think of several reasons why Reece Morgan could not be Lost Bullet, but as he thought about them, each one turned to dust.

The receptionist had a full head of hair and a beard. Yet earlier today Owen had joked that Luke should use a false beard and hair to change his own appearance. Obviously, Morgan had come up with the same simple idea. And it had worked beautifully because Luke hadn't recognized him among the Visionaries.

"He's been clever," Luke admitted. "On Tuesday he left a message saying he was feeling bad and that he'd gone to see his doctor. No God-fearing Visionary would do that. It was a good way of putting me off the scent."

"Note also that his absence from the hotel coincided with the attack on the Pairing Committee."

Luke nodded. "Yes. I was trying to figure out if I'd seen Morgan walking with a limp, but I've only ever seen him behind the reception desk. I've never even seen his legs. And then there's Elodie, the maid. She's the key, you know. You wouldn't expect a Visionary to work alongside a white, but I bet he put up with it so he could get information from her. She'd have made it easy for him. Whenever she asked for time off from work, I bet he'd act interested and ask her what she was doing. He'd soon find out where whites lived and when they got together."

Luke was fixed to the spot in the corridor, his brain in overdrive. "Last Friday, after I joined the Church—you know, when I came back in a sweat—Morgan was already at the desk. Fast work. But if he was one of the Visionaries who left the meeting right away, I guess he'd have had the time to make himself a receptionist again. He'd have been at it while I was talking to the others. And when I got back to the hotel, he said something about having just arrived for duty." Luke closed his eyes and murmured, "Morgan, huh?" Then he opened his eyes wide. "Malc, I've got to go back to the hotel right now. I want you to get your nice new electrons into some databases there." Breaking his thoughts, he ran for the exit at full speed. "Did they get a bullet out of you?"

"Confirmed. The agents also found three cartridge cases on top of the elevator."

"Have they been examined?"

"Confirmed."

"It's definitely you, Malc. Still answering questions without telling me what I really want to know. What were the results?"

"They match the bullets and cartridge cases found at the London Pairing Committee room and the Hammersmith Fertility Clinic."

"Of course!" Moving into top gear, Luke said, "Before we go back, can you plug yourself into London's health records?"

"I can access The Authorities' files by radio contact in this building."

"Good. Search all medical databases. Did Reece Morgan have an appointment at any doctor's office or hospital in the last week?"

"Processing."

Luke reached the door, but before he went out he waited for Malc to report.

"There is no record of Reece Morgan seeking medical advice."

"I didn't think so."

Just as Luke was about to push open the door, Malc said, "I will go first."

"Why?"

"Because Reece Morgan may be out there, and you are not bulletproof."

"Neither are you."

"I can be repaired or replaced easily."

Luke laughed. "Is your sense of déjà vu still in one piece?"

"With a perfect memory, I do not have . . ."

"Yeah. All right, all right. Out you go—into a hail of bullets."

There were no gunshots when Malc went outside and scanned the area. The bank of the Thames river was alive with rats. The surge of water had probably displaced them from their usual haunts. The ambushed autobarge had been removed, and in the middle of the flow another heavily laden barge was heading automatically for the Midlands. None of the people in view seemed to be threatening. As Luke stepped out with Malc, he felt secure again. At least, he felt as safe as it was possible to feel in London.

"You've still got laser capability, don't you?" asked Luke.

"Confirmed."

"Let's hope, next time, you get a chance to use it."

Malc soon had an opportunity to fire his laser. Luke didn't want to announce his presence in the Central Hotel, so Malc burned through the mechanism on the emergency exit at the back of the building, and they slipped into the hotel unnoticed.

Inside the apartment Malc logged on to the hotel records and searched for Reece Morgan's work schedule.

While Malc went through the database Luke said, "To tell the truth, I feel like a fool. There I was trying to act like a good Visionary, and Morgan had his eye on me all along. He must have known what I was up to."

Malc interrupted Luke's thoughts. "I have cross-checked the times of all of the murders, the arson at Clement School, and meetings of The World Church of Eternal Vision with Morgan's working hours. On every occasion he was not in the hotel."

"Makes sense," Luke replied. "Is he on duty now?"

"No. He will arrive within the next hour for the night shift."

"Yeah. I guess he will. He'll act normal because he thinks he destroyed you—and the evidence of his identity." Luke swallowed and then added, "To make sure, he might come for me."

"Speculation but well-founded."

Luke let out a long breath. "Right. I know where I go from here. To his house. Find his address, Malc. The hotel's bound to have it on file somewhere. We'll go tonight while he's on duty here. That'll keep me out of his sight, and it'll finish the case off if I can get my hands on his rifle."

"You should not contaminate fingerprint evidence."

But there was a problem. Half an hour after Morgan should have reported for duty he had still not arrived at the hotel.

Luke sighed again. "He knows we're on to him. He's the cautious type, so he's keeping his distance." He hesitated and then made up his mind. "We'll go to his quarters anyway. It's too good an opportunity to wrap up the whole thing. It's just that . . . Morgan could be getting back at me. He'll know that I need to search his home, so he might've set his own trap. And I could be walking right into it." Luke shook his head and stood up. "Come on. An FI's got to do what an FI's got to do."

"That is self-evident," Malc responded, "and it means nothing."

"It means I'm putting us in the line of fire again."

Chapter Twenty-Five

It was a shabby place on Tottenham Court Corridor. Luke should have guessed. It was almost certainly where Lost Bullet had dropped the piece of paper bearing the Church's previous address and then shot at Owen Goode. He'd opened fire because Owen had caught the paper and because he was white. No doubt, Morgan had tried to follow Owen but, with his damaged leg, failed to keep up. Instead he'd gone to Thomas's Hospital and taken out his anger on Dr. Suleman.

The outdoor lamps provided only a little light. In semidarkness Luke approached Morgan's overgrown home carefully, darting from tree to tree with Malc at his side. He'd hide behind a trunk while Malc scanned the walkway ahead and suggest the next spot that would provide cover. Luckily, Malc did not need visible light. He wasn't restricted to a human's narrow range of wavelengths. He also trained his sensors on the walls of the two-story house, concentrating on the darkened windows, but he did not detect the metal of a rifle barrel among the ivy, elder, and clematis.

Reaching the front door at last, Luke unlocked it and allowed Malc to poke around inside. After the mobile declared it to be free of adults and weapons Luke entered. The only sign of life was a little girl sitting on the narrow staircase. Luke squatted down in front of her and said very quietly, "Do you know Mr. Morgan?"

She nodded and pointed upstairs.

Still whispering, Luke asked, "Is he here, do you know?"

The girl shrugged.

The door across from the bottom of the staircase opened, and right away Malc flew in front of Luke.

The girl's father looked surprised and even angry. Scowling at Luke, he came out, picked up his daughter, and, without a word, whisked her away and into the ground-floor apartment.

With Malc scouting ahead of him, Luke began to climb the stairs. Halfway up, they turned a corner. Luke did not expect Lost Bullet to be hiding around the corner because a light was on somewhere above. If Morgan planned an ambush there, he would surely have turned off the lamp. Malc confirmed that the landing was clear, so Luke tiptoed to the top of the flight of stairs and then to the door of Morgan's quarters. In a hushed voice he said, "I'll unlock it and push it open. Okay? I'll stand on this side, and you take the other. Then you go in and scan everywhere. If he's there, disable him before he disables you. If he's not, turn on the lights. I'll wait."

To Luke, it seemed like cruelty. Malc had only just recovered from being shot, and Luke was asking him to

face the same man and the same rifle. At least Malc could not experience trauma. While Malc performed his heroics, Luke stayed behind a wall. He was no coward, but he felt like one.

He got out his identity card and placed it against the security panel. The door clicked but stayed shut. Luke glanced at Malc and nodded before giving the door a shove and flattening himself against the landing wall.

When the door slid back, no light shone from inside. The place was in darkness. Either Morgan was not there, or he was pretending not to be at home. Malc went into the apartment and began a thorough scan.

Outside Luke propped himself against the wall and tried to keep his heart and stomach under control. He knew that Malc was taking most of the risks, but even so, he was anxious. Reece Morgan could have anticipated this visit. He could have figured out that Luke would wait on the landing while a repaired or different mobile searched his rooms. It struck Luke that Morgan could creep quietly up the stairs at any moment and open fire. While Malc swept the apartment, Luke kept an eye on the top part of the staircase. At the slightest sound or the first appearance of a bald head Luke would dart into Morgan's quarters and slam the door shut.

When Malc came out, Luke almost jumped out of his skin.

"The living room, bedroom, kitchen, and bathroom are unoccupied. A door into another room is barred to me. An infrared scan shows that it is warmer than its surroundings. Therefore, it is a highly heated room."

Luke frowned. "Okay. Let's go in."

The living room, bedroom, and kitchen took Luke by surprise. For some reason, he expected them to be neat and clean, but they were a mess. Not lingering, he went to the final door and put his hand against it. Luke could not detect the warmth that was obvious to Malc's sensors. The door was fastened with some kind of mechanical lock. He whispered, "Zap it, Malc. Burn right through." Then he stood to one side and waited.

The living room filled with the smell of burning wood, and a trail of blue smoke came from the spot that Malc had targeted. After three or four minutes the door swung inward by a few inches, and Malc switched off his laser.

Malc moved against the door and slowly pushed it open. As he did so, a shaft of intense blue-white light came into the living room, making the smoke particles shimmer. The mobile had discovered an indoor greenhouse. Poppies were growing under a sunlamp, and in one corner of the room an electric fire belted out heat. In another, there was a bench stocked with chemical equipment.

Luke stood in the doorway, shaking his head and

smiling with relief. "This is where he cultivates his painkilling plants, extracts the morphine, and purifies it."

"Correct," Malc agreed. "By visual inspection, these plants are *Papaver somniferum*."

Luke turned around. "The rest of the place is a pigsty."

"Incorrect," Malc said. "Pigs do not sit in chairs."

"Hey," Luke replied, "that's almost a joke. Have you got new programming—a humor chip?"

"It was not a joke," he said. "It is a fact."

"All right. Let's get down to work. We'll need some agents in here to bag everything up, but scan around for anything relevant, like a rifle."

Luke put on his medical gloves and pushed open the bathroom door. Stunned, he halted in the entrance. Unlike the rest of the apartment, it was immaculate. Every surface gleamed with cleanliness. All down the left-hand side was a dressing area with a spotless mirror that covered the full width of the wall. On the long dressing table there were two plastic models of human heads wearing wigs of black hair. In a tray there were four false mustaches of different lengths and styles, eyelashes, and even fake eyebrows. Tweezers, makeup, nail clippers, and a shaving kit had been arranged lovingly around a picture of God.

"Malc! You've got some recording to do. There might

be enough in here for a conviction."

After half an hour of searching the apartment Luke and Malc failed to find his rifle. They did come across a knit cap and a couple of coats with hoods. Morgan had probably used one of them when he'd attacked the Pairing Committee.

"Get some agents here to sort it all out, Malc, and have them seal the place. I can't hang around. I've got to get going. He's out there somewhere," Luke nodded toward the door. "On the run with a rifle. He's probably wandering around as Lost Bullet, not a respectable receptionist. That makes him a serious threat."

"You have had a message from the Central Hotel," Malc announced.

"Oh?"

"You have a visitor waiting there."

Suddenly wary, Luke asked, "Who?"

"Ethan Loach."

"Ethan Loach," Luke repeated. "I'm not sure whether I should see him or not. But . . . I'm curious. It might be risky, but I'll go and see what he's up to."

"I must be with you," Malc said.

"Agreed. This time I wouldn't dream of keeping you out of it. Maximum defense mode."

Chapter Twenty-Six

It was late—after ten o'clock—when Luke invited Ethan into his quarters. Luke did not feel like an investigator interviewing a witness. He felt more like a student up before a feared instructor. On edge, he said, "What can I do for you?"

Dressed as always in a dark suit, stiff white shirt, and red tie, Ethan sat down across from Luke without being asked and pulled his chair close. He leaned forward, bringing his bald head close to Luke. "Reece Morgan contacted me. He complained about you harassing him. He says you are not a true Visionary."

Luke stared at the carpet for a few seconds. His job at The World Church of Eternal Vision was over. He did not have to pretend anymore. He looked up into Ethan's face and said, "I'm leaving the Church. I never had faith."

Ethan smiled. He almost laughed. "I know. That's why I sedated the snake."

"What?"

"I'm not a fool, Luke. And I have to say you're a brave boy. Much braver than your age. After all, you didn't know the snake was half asleep."

Luke was astonished and puzzled. "Why?"

"I suspected that one of our flock was veering from the straight and narrow. But I couldn't be seen to doubt them all—or test them all. That would have torn us apart. I was waiting for God to send us an FI to narrow it down and help me see the light. It was only a matter of time. You were chosen to infiltrate the Church. I didn't realize God would pick someone so young, though."

Luke couldn't reply. He thought that he'd duped Ethan, but Ethan had been taking advantage of him all along.

"Is it Reece?" Ethan asked. "Is he the one?"

Luke waved toward Malc because mobiles always told the truth.

"No," Ethan snapped, angry for the first time. "I want to hear it from one of God's creations, from God's choice. And I want to watch you while you tell me. I want to see your eyes. Is Reece Morgan guilty of murder?"

Luke took a deep breath. "Yes. He killed three members of the London Pairing Committee on Tuesday and two medics at the Hammersmith Fertility Clinic a few days later. He probably killed Dr. Anna Suleman as well, but I have no proof of that. He's out of control."

Ethan did not hesitate. He nodded and said, "I believe you. I should have realized. A while ago he broke a bone in his foot when he fell. It never healed completely, so God was punishing him for something. Maybe he was hatching his evil plans. I should have picked up on that."

"Do you know where he is now?"

"No. But I can guess."

"Where?" asked Luke.

Ethan pulled back and shook his head. "I will speak to him first. I owe him that."

Less nervous now, Luke said, "You won't warn him to stay away?"

The Visionary leader stood up. "Not if I look in his eyes and see sin. No. I'll send you a message, tell you where to go to find him."

"But . . ."

"I'm a man of my word, Investigator Harding." With that, he turned and left Luke's room.

There was little that Luke could do except wait. After all, London was a big city with untold numbers of hiding places. Reece Morgan could be in any of them. Yet Luke trusted that Ethan Loach would keep his word.

Luke was too hyped up for sleep. He tried to contact Jade, but he got only a message telling him that she had gone to a club with her northern friends. Instead of chatting to her, Luke filled the apartment with her music and went through all of the evidence for the case, checking with Malc which items were admissible. The exercise made him realize that, to be absolutely sure of a conviction, he still needed Lost Bullet's rifle. He had little doubt that, wherever Reece Morgan was, he'd have the weapon with him.

The idea made Luke feel guilty. He should have warned Ethan that Reece Morgan was armed. It was possible that Morgan would kill Ethan, walk away, and then disappear into the sprawling squalor of the South. Yet, when Luke thought about Ethan Loach, he did not despair. He suspected that the Church leader was not the type of man to be shot. He was too formidable. And he would show no fear because he had faith that his God would protect him.

Luke's mind swirled with issues of treachery and trust. He put down an evidence bag and turned to Malc. "I'm really sorry that I left you in that elevator."

"There is no need for an apology. It was the only logical course of action."

"But . . ." Luke sighed. "But what if Owen had been shot? Would I have run away then?"

"Insufficient information. However, an objective assessment of the situation would support withdrawal."

It was no use. Luke was talking about trust, and Malc was restricted to logic. "It didn't seem right to leave you. Were you hurt? I don't suppose so."

"I cannot be hurt because I do not have a nervous system. You should not think of me as humanoid."

"I suppose there's an advantage to being a machine when the bullets begin to fly and someone runs out on you."

Malc knew nothing about pain or loneliness or guilt. Equally, Luke realized, he never felt joy or togetherness or compassion. To Malc, Jade's music was merely a sequence of frequencies at different volumes. He could not be moved by it. Jade's face was a contoured structure that could be measured and recognized. He could not be attracted to it. Her perfume was a collection of molecules that could be analyzed and identified. The smell could not trigger emotion in Malc.

Getting back to the case, Luke asked, "Have you passed our conclusions to The Authorities?"

"Confirmed."

"I hope that they're happy."

"They await the arrest of Reece Morgan."

"They're not the only ones," Luke replied.

It was not until Monday afternoon that Ethan Loach's imposing features formed on Luke's telescreen. Eagerly, Luke jumped to his feet. "Yes? What news?"

"First things first, my friend. I have spoken to Reece."

"And?" Luke prompted.

Ethan sighed. "It seems you're not the only one living a lie. I never knew he worked at your hotel and wore a disguise. He didn't want to advertise his allegiance to the Church. That smacks of shame or guilt. He also confessed to murder, including the doctor last Monday. Killing is a sin, even if the victims are themselves the worst type of sinners."

A confession to anybody but Malc was useless to the law. "Where is he?"

"He's retreated into the Church. Charing Cross Cab Station."

"If I go now, will he be there?" Luke asked eagerly. "You haven't given him a reason to run away?"

"No. He's unlikely to move on. He's made it his home."

"You didn't let on that you'd tell me?"

"No."

"Thank you."

"God be with you, Luke Harding."

The sun had gone down by the time that Luke and Malc reached the entrance to Charing Cross Cab Station. While Luke stared into the gaping hole, an empty electric cab pulled out of the waiting area to his left and took off down the ramp that led into the tunnel under the Thames river. Luke took a deep breath and turned toward the five guards that he'd requested as backup. "I'm going in," he said. "You stay here in case he gets past me somehow."

"You don't want us to check it out first?"

Yes, he did, but he wasn't going to admit it. He was determined to show The Authorities that he could wrap it up on his own—with Malc, of course. He had already placed Owen Goode in danger, and he wasn't going to put anyone else in the firing line. He would do his own dirty work. "No," he replied. "If he comes up here, trying to escape, stop him from getting away."

"We have been cleared to use all necessary force."

Luke nodded and then headed down the escalator. He tiptoed while Malc glided. The way to the old abandoned depot had a different atmosphere now that Malc was at his side. This time Luke was anxious about a madman with a rifle rather than the unknown. At the bottom of the static steps Malc checked out the first clammy passageway. "There is no human life," he reported. "A colony of bats is beginning to stir at the far end, and there are two foxes ahead, but that is all. Should I provide extra lighting?"

"No. I don't want to warn him that we're on our way."

The lights in the curved ceiling were enough to lead Luke through the stinking cave to the narrow tunnel on the right.

Luke nodded toward the tunnel and whispered, "Is he anywhere in there?"

"No."

Leaving behind the sound of dripping water, Luke started to walk carefully through the dark warren. Framed by the grubby walls on both sides, he felt very vulnerable. If Morgan appeared at the end with his rifle,

Luke could not get out of his line of fire. He could only turn around and sprint back to the main passage to find cover. But he doubted that he would get that far. The first bullet would floor Malc. The second would be his.

Trying to empty his mind of everything that could go wrong, he continued walking softly, aware that each time he put his weight on a foot, he walked on slushy litter and made a faint squelching noise. With each step, he crept closer to the underground hall, closer to Morgan's territory, and farther from safety. Subconsciously, he went slower and slower as he approached the bizarre church. His legs were faltering as his heart quickened.

With a few feet—perhaps 30 paces—to go, he squashed himself against the wall and beckoned to Malc. "This is it," he said in a barely audible voice. "If Ethan's right, he's just ahead. It opens out into a big space. Go in, silent mode, and watch out for yourself. Whatever you do, don't get shot. If you're taken down this time . . . I'm next. There's no easy way out from here."

"Confirmed," Malc replied at his lowest volume.

Chapter Twenty-Seven

Luke felt abandoned. Everything was completely quiet. Only a few seconds had passed, but it seemed like an eternity. At least a rifle's thunder had not ripped through the stagnant air. Luke could feel the cold against his back and dampness seeping into his shirt. It could have been sweat or moisture trickling down the wall.

Making Luke jump, Malc's profile appeared unannounced in the archway. Light glinted off his right side from one of the electric lamps set in the wall. He said, "Reece Morgan is here but is unconscious."

"What?" Luke lurched into the middle of the passage. "More light, Malc. Show me."

The mobile led the way into the derelict chamber of The World Church of Eternal Vision. His spotlight picked out the Visionary in the middle of the ring of workbenches and machines, like a fallen actor on a freakish stage. Next to him lay a golf bag with a rifle protruding from it.

Taking care of safety first, Luke put on disposable gloves and moved the weapon out of Reece Morgan's reach. It was almost certainly unnecessary. Morgan was helpless, not far from death.

He was dressed in his Church uniform of dark suit, light shirt, and red tie. Only his shaved head and hands were bared. And his face . . . it was almost unrecognizable. The right side was swollen and stretched as if it had been pumped up like a basketball. His eye had disappeared into the huge blister, surrounded by dead tissue that was turning black. He seemed to be paralyzed, but the muscles on the left side of his face were twitching uncannily and horribly. Blood-filled spots were appearing on his skin, and his left eye was stained red. The arteries and veins in his neck had ruptured, bruising his flesh and creating pools of blood under his skin. Occasionally he struggled to drag a mouthful of air into his fluid-filled lungs, gurgling through the liquids in his throat. It sounded like someone sucking the dregs of a drink through a straw.

Luke had seen the symptoms before. He knew exactly what had happened. Lost Bullet had been poisoned by rattlesnake venom. Because he'd admitted his sins to Ethan Loach, the preacher had put him through another rattlesnake test. Judging by the disfigurement of his face, the creature had bitten him on the right cheek. Like Sarah Toback before him, Reece Morgan had failed the Church's test.

"Malc, send out an emergency radio message to the antivenin unit at Thomas's Hospital. He needs antivenin for a rattlesnake bite. Now."

"Transmitting. However, it is highly unlikely to get here in time. Also it is illogical to strive to keep him

alive so that he can face the death penalty."

Luke looked up at Malc severely. "Well, that's the difference between you and me. He's a human being, and if there's a chance of saving him, I'll do it. And I'm just an FI, not a judge. It's my job to charge him with his crimes, not sentence him." He gazed down at the pitiful sight of Reece Morgan. "Is there anything we can do for him?"

"The site of the bite should be left alone. Current medical practice does not recommend attempting to suck out the venom. The only suggestion is removal of constrictions near the swelling."

Luke nodded. "You mean loosen his collar and tie."

"Confirmed."

When Luke leaned over him, undid his tie, and tried to undo the top button of his shirt, Morgan's left eye shifted as if he was aware of Luke's presence. There was terror in that eye. Luke ignored it. Morgan's neck was so bloated that his collar dug into his skin tightly. There was no slack to allow Luke to unfasten the button. "Laser, Malc. Burn the cotton or melt the button, whichever happens first."

Malc focused a red dot of light on the center of the button in order to guide the laser and then fired. After a few seconds the collar gave way. It was like a dam bursting. More fluids gushed into Morgan's bulging neck, but at least he seemed to take in air a little more easily. Before his almost still heart failed altogether his last breaths would not be so painful. Luke and Malc had eased his way out of the world.

Nodding toward the golf bag, Luke said, "Scan what you can see of the rifle and his hands, Malc. Have we got what we need to clinch the case?"

"His fingerprints are on the rifle."

"That'll do it then."

"Confirmed. You have sufficient evidence to charge Reece Morgan with multiple murder and attempted murder." Malc hesitated before adding, "You need to consider arresting Ethan Loach."

Luke shook his head. "I'd like to, but it won't work. Not for murder, anyway. Ethan didn't bite him. The snake did. And I bet Ethan didn't force him to face God's judgment. I doubt if anyone's ever refused the invitation to take the test, but I'm sure it was voluntary. You might as well put out a call to arrest the snake or God."

"Nonhumans and mythical creatures are outside the law."

"I know what Ethan Loach will be doing. He won't bring the Church back here again. He'll move on. Right now he'll be passing around another piece of paper with a new address." Luke sighed. "I'm done with Visionaries, but I'll help The Authorities round up the ones who've driven whites out of their homes and wrecked doctors' offices. They won't get them all, though, and they'll

never get rid of The World Church of Eternal Vision. There'll always be someone to carry it on."

Morgan stirred. His slow, erratic breathing had suddenly become noisier, more desperate. His open mouth seemed to be trying to form a final word. "Res . . . Resp . . ."

Luke looked at Malc. "Did the antivenin unit get the message?"

"Confirmed. A team is on its way."

But by the time that the medics arrived aboveground, Reece Morgan was beyond help. And beyond further punishment.

Want to find out about Luke Harding's exciting next case? Here is the first chapter of the next **Traces** *story,* **Roll Call.** *Read on for a taste of more forensic crime solving with Luke and Malc.*

Chapter One

Emily Wonder's eyes did not narrow when the dazzling sunshine fell across her face. Her numbed eyelids did not snap shut to protect her from the blinding light. Lying across the sofa, she was helpless against the unbearable pain in her eyes. Tears and sweat rolled down her cheeks and onto the soft cushion. She was not tied to the sofa, but she was completely unable to shift her position. However much she tried, she could not move an arm, a leg, her head, or any other part of her body. She could not even blink an eyelid. She just lay there in her apartment, tethered by invisible bonds, as if immobilized by an overwhelming weight, and waited to die.

It had been a good day until, feeling faint, she'd lain down on the sofa after lunch and become limp within minutes. First she'd felt a prickly sensation around her mouth. The tingling had spread pleasantly throughout her body, bringing a feeling of lazy warmth. But then came the shivering, the agonizing pins and needles in her fingertips, tongue, and nose, and the waves of nausea as her ailing nervous system shut down. Her mind remained agonizingly clear, though, as she realized that she was not suffering merely from heat exhaustion.

In this extraordinarily hot summer the weather was striving to turn the country into a desert. Reservoirs were running dry, and rivers were reduced to sad trickles. On the day of Emily's death Dundee sweltered. The ski center's exhausted air-conditioning system took its last breath and broke down. The indoor slope defrosted immediately, and the snow melted away. The Music Hall, Caird Theater, and McManus Art Gallery were packed with people seeking entertainment and an escape from the heat.

Along Riverside Walkway the tarmac was sticky underfoot. In the morning Emily hesitated as she strolled past the beautifully preserved sailing ships moored in the docks. For a few minutes she gazed at cabs speeding over the wide estuary on the impressive Tay Bridge. The iron railings divided the sunlight so that the cabs seemed to move under strobe lighting. It made their crossing appear jerky rather than smooth.

Just as she was about to continue her walk, an older woman bumped into her and muttered, "Oops. Sorry."

Emily shrugged. "That's okay." Even wearing sunglasses, she had to squint in the sunlight to get a good view of the person who had nudged her. But the woman had pulled a wide-brimmed hat down protectively over her eyes. Half of her face was in the shadow. Emily watched her walk slowly away. She was dressed in a short skirt and flimsy floral top. With every step, she placed one foot deliberately right in front of the other, giving her the flamboyant appearance of a fashion model.

Continuing along Riverside Walk, Emily visited Dundee Animal Sanctuary. There the vets were making garlic ice cream for the animals to keep them cool. For the first time, the amphibian house did not need power in order to maintain its tropical conditions. The yellow-splashed California newts and harlequin frogs were lapping up the sunshine. The aquarium and sea-life tanks had to be cooled to keep the water hospitable for the puffer fish, the tiny blue-ringed octopus, the garish angelfish, and the xanthid crabs.

Emily ate her lunch in the conservation park's restaurant. When she presented her identity card, the attendant asked a question that Emily had suffered 100 times before.

"Are you *the* Emily Wonder?"

Shaking her head and smiling, Emily pulled down her sunglasses and gave her usual response. "If I started to sing, you'd know right away that I'm not. I share a name with her, not a voice."

"That's a shame."

Eager to end the stale conversation, Emily began eating her salad.

Afterward, thinking that the heat was taking its toll on her, she got up to go straight home. Just as she got to the door, though, someone called her name. She turned to see a man dashing up to her.

He was shorter than Emily but older. He had a big, bushy beard, and even inside, he was wearing a cap. Under its rim, his eyes were intense. His left arm was encased in a cast and was hooked across his chest.

She had never seen him before in her life. Startled, Emily stepped back, and her bare arm touched one of the cacti on a shelf. The plant's sharp spines pierced her skin. "Ouch!"

The man glanced at the large, flat cactus with clumps of brown spines and then looked into Emily's face. "You're all right. Just a sting. It's not poisonous."

Rubbing the spot where the prickles had scratched her, she said, "What do you want? How do you know my name?"

The strange man held out her identity card in his right palm. "You left it on the table."

"Oh. Silly me. Thank you," she replied, taking it from him. Feeling light-headed, she opened the door and continued toward her apartment.

The sun executed an arc high up in the clear sky, and

the vertical blinds in Emily's window chopped the harsh light into bands of shade and brilliance, turning her living room into a cage with dark bars that shifted throughout the afternoon. Emily could have counted the hours by the alternate periods of welcome shade and tortuous glare on her inert face. So much perspiration cascaded from her body that she felt like she'd just walked through a rainstorm. Her muscles were paralyzed, but her brain was fully aware that she was about to die from inevitable heart failure or suffocation. Robbed of speech and motion, there was nothing she could do about it. She was defenseless against the unknown and unseen poison that had penetrated every part of her body except her mind. Cruelly, the chemical could not cross into her brain, so she remained completely conscious.

For seven hours Emily experienced her young life slipping slowly away. For seven hours she was a zombie—alive and awake, yet, to all intents and purposes, lifeless.

She was aware of time passing and the pain of her organs failing one by one, but she was not aware that she had been murdered.

The forensic investigator assigned to Emily's death also did not realize that she had been murdered. A thorough examination of her body did not reveal any evidence of a crime. Even the pathologist who conducted the autopsy did not find the true cause of death. The toxicity tests on her blood were negative. The microscopic puncture wounds and inflammation on her left forearm were trivial, caused by the tiny spines of a prickly pear cactus, *Opuntia vulgaris*. All of her internal organs had been healthy when they had suddenly ceased to function. The pathologist put her death down to heart failure as a result of unknown natural causes.

Without a trace of unlawful killing, The Authorities closed the case.